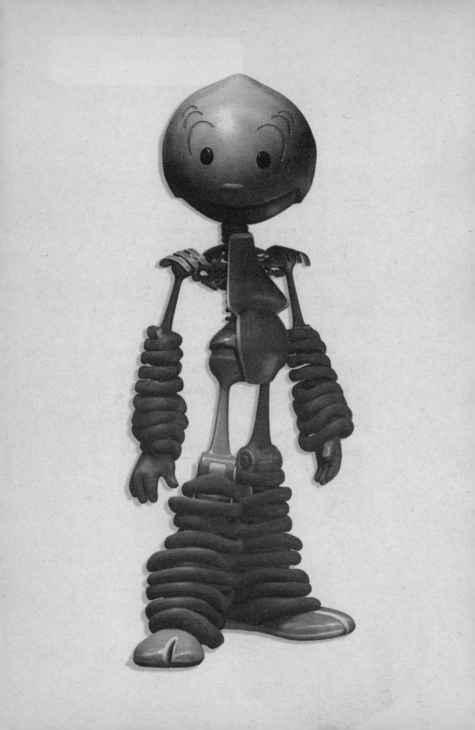

EAGER

HELEN FOX

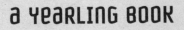

a YEARLING BOOK

With love and thanks

for John—this book would not have happened without you
and
for Kay Collison, a remarkable teacher, who encouraged me
to be me

PROLOGUE

EGR3 stood in the small dark room and watched the sea. It tumbled and roared below him. The spray rose so high it threatened to touch him, but the wind carried it away before it could reach that far. The sky was black and lowering, and the sea a cauldron of gray. He could taste something familiar. What was it? Salt.

The room itself was at the top of the house, tucked under the eaves. The light on the landing had been left on and a thin beam peeked under the door. Otherwise, the only light was the pale glow of a streetlamp through the curtainless window.

EGR3 had spent nearly all his life in the room. Yet he had traveled through the streets of the city, climbed steps and hills. He had run in the woods, dodging fallen logs and holes that showed themselves at the last moment. He had stood in awe, looking up at great trees and listening to the murmuring of their leaves and the creaking of their branches. He had walked up and down trains and hoverbuses, keeping his balance as they tipped and turned or sped over bumps. He had practiced chopping wood and threading needles, pouring water and moving heavy objects. And all the time his brain was asking, and comparing, and cataloging, and storing away the experiences.

A gust of wind knocked him off balance and he hastily stepped back from the edge of the cliff. He heard the door of the room slide open. A human would not have heard, but EGR3's hearing was as sharp as an owl's.

"Good evening, Professor," he said, turning toward the door just in time to glimpse a luminous ball as it floated across the landing and out of sight. The professor, a stocky man with unruly white hair, came into the room and smiled a broad smile. It surprised and delighted EGR3, rather as the sudden appearance of the sun had thrilled him, the first time he had seen it rise.

"Good evening, EGR3. And how are you tonight?"

"I'm on the edge of a cliff," replied EGR3, who understood the question to be about his progress. "Looking down on the sea." A hoverbus skirted the window, plunging them into darkness. It moved slowly by, and light seeped into the room again.

"And are you going to go down to the sea?" asked the professor.

"Oh, no!" exclaimed EGR3. "It's much too rough. Besides, if I try to climb down the cliff I may fall and break something. And if I step over the edge I will . . . be destroyed." He stopped, an unfamiliar sensation rising inside him.

The professor nodded. "Go on."

"The cliff edge is uneven. It is possible that I might lose my footing. Or the ground might give way. The edge is too dangerous. I will step back."

The professor moved further into the room. EGR3 could see his eyes clearly now in the light from the window.

"EGR3." The professor's voice was soft. "I believe you are ready." He looked intently at him for a moment, then walked toward the door.

"Professor?"

"Yes?" He stepped back into the room and EGR3 could see his face once more.

"Your eyes. The look they have. Is that what you call a 'kind' expression?"

The corners of the professor's mouth turned slightly upward. "I hope so, EGR3. . . . Yes, yes, it is."

He turned again and was gone, the door sliding gently behind him.

CHAPTER 1

The Bell family lived in the suburbs, in a house built of glass and steel, designed by Mr. Bell. Their neighbors in Wynston Avenue, who also lived in glass houses, had planted tall dense hedges to shield them from view. Mr. and Mrs. Bell said what was the point of a beautiful house if no one else could enjoy it, and built themselves a low brick wall. However, they liked their privacy as much as anyone, and it was fortunate that the house was secluded by being set on a bend in the road. There was also a huge lime tree in the front garden that veiled one side of the building.

The center of the house was an atrium, paved with brick and full of plants and flowers. A wide hallway opening onto it connected the ground-floor rooms. There was a half-landing with an office, exercise room and study area; bedrooms and bathrooms were on the top floor. The land at the back was divided into grass, a vegetable garden and a slightly wild overgrown patch at the far end.

As dawn approached, the birds in the lime tree began their

chorus. A gray cat slinked across the lawn and over the brick wall. Seconds later the house swept a sensor around the garden for the hundredth time that night to check for intruders. It took the outside temperature and barometric pressure. Today was going to be a mild day with the possibility of a light shower before the evening.

A noise downstairs alerted the house that someone was up. It turned on its electronic eye in the kitchen and saw that the butler was at work. He was chopping something on a large wooden board and talking to the kettle.

Room by room, the house checked its occupants. Fleur Bell was buried so deeply in the duvet that it was impossible to tell which way up she was. The house zoomed in somewhere about her middle to reassure itself that she was still breathing. Satisfied that the duvet was gently rising and falling, the house turned its eye to the bedroom next door. Fleur's younger brother, Gavin Bell, was sprawled across the bed, the covers thrown off as if he had been wrestling in his sleep. Normal, concluded the house promptly, with barely a glance at him.

Charlotte Bell, lying in a cot in the nursery, was twitching in her sleep. No cause for alarm there. In the main bedroom Mr. and Mrs. Bell looked comfortable enough, but Mr. Bell was muttering to himself and the house considered that he might have a fever. It looked for other symptoms, found none, and decided that he was nearing the end of a dream cycle.

The hours passed and the house grew busier—waking everyone up and setting the temperature for showers and baths. It checked the gobetween for news that might interest the Bells, adjusted roof panels to create more heat and raised the blinds on the day ahead.

Gavin was the first to come downstairs. He was in a bad mood, though he didn't know why. It felt as if his body had been given a good shake and parts of him had fallen back into the wrong place. He had been looking forward to today. After home study he was going to the learning center for a game of liveball. That was the good bit. On the other hand, he was sure he had instructed the house to wake him with his favorite music; instead, a shrill voice had screeched "Wakey! Wakey!" in his ear. He hadn't had breakfast yet, and he had a nagging feeling that his mum and dad were going to have one of their Discussions. He jumped the final steps and burst into the dining room, his shirt half undone and one of his socks twisted.

"Where is everyone?"

"Your mother is in the shower and your father is changing Charlotte's nappy," replied the house in a soothing, feminine voice. "Your sister is—"

"All right," snapped Gavin. "I didn't really expect an answer. It was a rit . . . ret . . ."

"Rhetorical question?" prompted the house.

"Yes, I know." Gavin sat down to adjust his sock. "Anyway, you're not supposed to be on in here. You know Mum doesn't like machines in the dining room."

"I am not a machine," corrected the house.

"Yes you are, drybrain. You just don't have a body." He looked up. "Go on then, turn yourself off."

There was a long pause before the green light beside the door began to flicker, and an even longer pause before it went out. Gavin frowned. He knew that machines were not supposed to have personalities, apart from the one people might choose for them. But if anyone had asked him, he would have said that the house was stubborn and sulky.

His father came into the room carrying the baby and placed her in the high chair. Gavin kissed Charlotte on the forehead. Normally, he didn't do a lot of kissing, but his little sister was an exception. Charlotte craned her neck to look at him and chuckled, revealing a dimple and a row of tiny white teeth.

"Morning," said Mr. Bell. He was wearing a high-necked jacket and slim-legged trousers. A narrow piece of cloth poked up behind the collar of the jacket.

"Morning, Dad. You look interesting."

"Interesting?" said Mr. Bell.

Gavin eyed his father up and down. "Well, like something out of the twentieth century. All you need is a watch on your wrist instead of a jinn, and a top hat."

"Top hats are Victorian, I think you'll find. I've a very important meeting today and I think I look very smart."

Gavin's dad hardly ever dressed up. He worked with a lot of other architects who also looked most of the time as if they had just got out of bed.

"I'm meeting the top people at LifeCorp," he continued. "We're going to build them a new factory."

"Euphoric, Dad! Congratulations. But how come they've chosen you? I don't remember you mentioning it."

Mr. Bell looked guilty. He tied a bib around Charlotte's neck and sat down beside her. "I didn't," he admitted. "They held a competition to choose the architects last summer. We were asked not to tell anyone but since we've won we can hardly keep it a secret anymore. Now, I wonder what's for breakfast?"

Gavin had a sneaking feeling his father was changing the subject. They examined the dining table. "Bowls and side plates," mused Mr. Bell. "Well, that doesn't look too ominous."

The door slid open and Mrs. Bell and Fleur entered. They too stared at the table.

"Cereal and toast. That's OK," said Fleur with relief.

His mum kissed Gavin. "Morning," she murmured. "Did you sleep well?"

He wondered whether to tell her about the house screeching in his ear and decided not to. It would be just like her to go back to alarm clocks, or to volunteer to wake him herself. At least with the house he could tell it to let him snooze for ten minutes.

They joined Mr. Bell at the table.

"Dad's going to build a new factory for LifeCorp," Gavin told his sister.

"Really?" said Fleur. "Whereabouts?"

"Don't get excited," their father said. "It's on the edge of the city. I was hoping it might be somewhere exotic like Italy or Tanzania so I'd be allowed to travel."

The door opened and the butler rolled into the room, to an accompaniment of squeaks and whirrs.

"Good evening," he said in a gravelly voice.

Fleur and Gavin exchanged looks of alarm.

"Actually, Grumps . . . ," began Mr. Bell.

A ring indicated that the food lift had arrived. Mr. Bell left his sentence unfinished. The butler creaked his way toward the lift and took out a large tureen.

"Soup is served," he announced, setting down the tureen in the center of the table.

"Soup!" echoed Fleur. "For breakf—?"

"Shhh," said her mum. "You'll hurt his feelings. Thank you, Grumps."

"Tomato soup," intoned the butler. He lifted the lid. Steam wafted up and the unmistakable smell of cooked tomatoes filled the room.

The family stared in silence at the tureen. Grumps waited patiently, the lid in his hand.

"Perhaps a ladle?" said Mrs. Bell at last. "And some cereal and a yogurt for Charlotte."

"I forgot. I am most sorry." The butler replaced the lid and trundled out of the door. They heard him squeaking down the hallway.

"He doesn't have any feelings, Chloe," Mr. Bell said to his wife. "He's a machine."

"You know what I think," she retorted. "Grumps cares for us just like one of the family."

"He's programmed to care for us. The fridge cares for us too by looking after our food, but we don't get sentimental about it." Mr. Bell was growing a little tetchy, as he often did when they had this conversation.

This was exactly the Discussion that Gavin had feared. He wondered how far it would go today.

"My digestion cannot possibly tolerate the odor of soup at this hour," Gavin said grandly. "Why can't we have cereal too?" He looked at the clock on the wall. "It's eight o'clock. Eight o'clock in the morning!"

"It's only a vegetable," said his mother.

"Or a fruit," said Fleur. "Tomatoes are both."

"Chloe," urged Mr. Bell. "We really can't go on like this. . . ."

The door opened and Grumps entered with Charlotte's food, a ladle and a plate of bread rolls. He put the rolls on the table with a flourish. "Hot," he said, "with the compliments of the oven."

"We'd like some jam," said Fleur.

"Jam?"

Mr. Bell looked up from feeding Charlotte. "And marmalade," he added.

"Very well," said the butler, "if that's what you want." He looked inquiringly at Mrs. Bell.

She nodded and he went out. Gavin buried his head in his hands. "Bread and jam," he groaned. "What kind of a breakfast is that?"

"A perfectly respectable one," replied his mother. "Please sit up straight. And pass me your bowl."

Gavin's jaw dropped as his mother ladled tomato soup into his bowl. He would have liked to protest but he knew her too well. She could be very funny where Grumps was concerned.

"Just a small bowl for me, please," said Fleur in a small voice. "I'm not feeling very hungry."

Gavin shot her a look. Mrs. Bell tipped the hot scarlet liquid into her own bowl, then handed the ladle to her husband.

"Umm," she said, "makes a nice change. Especially on a chilly spring day."

"Actually, it's warm today. I just checked the weather and pollution levels on the gobey," said Fleur.

Her mum ignored her. "In lots of countries, soup is a common food for breakfast. India, for example."

"My friend Sarupa in Bombay has cornflakes," declared Fleur.

Mr. Bell dropped the ladle in the tureen with a clatter. "We need to talk about this. . . ."

Grumps entered with a collection of jars on a silver tray.

"Jam," he declared, "and marmalade."

Gavin seized one of the jars and unscrewed the lid. "Euphoric! Rations arrive just in time to save the starving troops."

"Will there be anything else?" Grumps stood stiffly in the doorway. Everyone's attention turned to Charlotte, who was swinging her bowl above her head.

"No, thank you," said Mrs. Bell distractedly.

Grumps exited. Mr. Bell took the bowl from Charlotte and placed it gingerly in front of her. Mrs. Bell put down her spoon and looked at her family around the table. "All right," she sighed. "I give in."

CHAPTER 2

Grumps stood in the kitchen and looked at his vegetable pie. He had made it as a main course to follow the tomato soup, but he had an inkling that it would not be welcome in the dining room. This was not the first time the family had failed to show their usual enthusiasm for his meals. There was something amiss and it troubled him.

"I'm getting old, of course," he told his friend, the kettle, which sat next to the sink. He began to sweep vegetable peelings into the waste-disposal unit. "When I was launched onto the market—fifteen years ago that is—I was the very latest model. The butler. We were all butlers in those days, or housekeepers. We weren't the first robots, of course. Did you know, we go back to the twentieth century? My ancestors used to assemble cars and television sets. They couldn't think, mind you. Not as you can," he added kindly. "They just did the same repetitive task. We were the first who could do everything— move, talk, think, reason, learn . . ." His voice trailed off. The light on the kettle flashed on.

"Hello!" chirped the kettle. "How many cups do you require?"

"The first fully automated household robot, that was me," continued Grumps. "Of course, it's all changed. The world does, you know. No one wants old-fashioned domestic servants anymore. They want robots to be 'personal assistants' or even friends!" He turned off the waste-disposal unit.

"I am plumbed into the main water supply and can fill myself automatically," trumpeted the kettle. "How many cups do you require?"

Grumps went to check whether the vegetable pie had cooled. It had not been long in the oven before he took it out, but the pie dish had been very hot to the touch. The green light by the door came on.

"Grumps," said the house, "you are needed in the dining room. That baby once again has thrown away its bowl."

Grumps decided against the robot cleaner for such a small job and went to fetch a dustpan and floor cloth.

"By the way," remarked the house, "I've been listening to the family. They're talking about getting rid of you." It turned its attention back to the Bells.

The dining room was still buzzing with talk. Now that Mrs. Bell had agreed that there was a problem with Grumps, everyone was determined to find a solution. It was not proving an easy task.

"Switch off," said Gavin, noticing the green light by the door.

"I just want to tell you that *he's* on his way," said the house. "In my opinion, you should go ahead and replace him. What good is he with a broken timer? He doesn't know whether it's noon or night, or what day of the week it is, for that matter."

"You could have told him!" said Gavin accusingly.

"The house is right," said Fleur. "Breakfast was a fiasco. We can't be telling him the time every five minutes."

Mr. Bell intervened. "We've agreed we can't go on like this, which means we need to buy a new robot. The question remains, what do we do with Grumps?"

The door opened before anyone had a chance to reply and the butler appeared. To his surprise they were sitting around the table exactly as he had left them. Perhaps they were waiting for the main course after all. Then he noticed that they were looking at him with an expression he did not recognize.

"We've picked up most of it," said Mrs. Bell, indicating the mess on the floor.

"Do you require anything more to eat?"

"No, thank you."

"Something smells good," said Gavin.

"I have made your favorite vegetable pie. And the pudding that Miss Fleur is so fond of."

Mrs. Bell's face softened and she looked meaningfully round the table at her family. "We'll have them tonight. Thank you."

There was a silence as Grumps registered Mrs. Bell's words. His heavy steel features took on a downcast expression. "I have failed again, haven't I?"

Mrs. Bell shifted in her seat. "It's your timer. You know it doesn't work properly. You must ask the house when you're confused."

"I didn't know I was confused," said the butler in a doleful tone. "These dark mornings and evenings—I get muddled."

"We'd have you repaired if we could," said Mr. Bell. "But your timer is so deep in your wiring that it could damage your entire system."

There was another pause, punctuated by sweeping sounds as Grumps cleaned the floor. He straightened up, the dustpan in his hand. "I am obsolete," he said matter-of-factly.

"That's ridiculous!" exclaimed Mrs. Bell.

"You could replace me with a model that is five times . . ." He reconsidered. ". . . Three times more efficient than I am."

"You function perfectly well. Apart from the minor problem of your timer . . . Why should we replace you, you're one of the family! You've been with us since we were married."

"I should not mind going to the scrapheap," went on Grumps. "After all, I should have no knowledge of it, once you removed my batteries."

Fleur looked at Gavin and rolled her eyes. He pretended not to notice.

"Go back to the kitchen, Grumps," said Mr. Bell. "We'll come and talk to you later."

Fleur put her hand to her forehead. "I shan't mind going to the scrapheap!" she mimicked. "Oh, I can't bear it. It's too, too tragic!"

"We humans don't last forever," said Mr. Bell to his wife, "and neither do machines. There's some truth in what he says."

"I hope you don't send *me* to the scrapheap if a part of me wears out," retorted Mrs. Bell. "He's not any old machine! He's a caring, thinking, feeling machine."

"It was kind of him to make our favorite food," said Gavin.

His dad sighed. "It isn't kindness—he's simply designed to repeat the things that please us. Look, just because Grumps can hold a conversation it doesn't mean he actually understands things like we do. He might behave like a human or an animal but it isn't real. He can't feel anything. He has no imagination, no emotions, no likes and dislikes."

Although Fleur had never really thought about it before, she wished she could agree with her dad. Life was difficult enough without having to consider the feelings of robots. Yet he was wrong.

"Grumps does have likes and dislikes. You can tell he doesn't get on with the house but he's very fond of the kettle."

"Well, he has preferences," said her dad. "The manufacturers programmed him that way to give him a bit of character. But it's like a cat who prefers a particular cushion, it doesn't mean much."

"If you're going to compare a robot to an animal . . . ," began Mrs. Bell.

"Animals are alive, Mum," said Gavin gently. "Robots are just machines that run on an energy supply."

Once again Fleur felt obliged to correct her family's grasp of the facts. "Animals need an energy supply too. They get theirs from food."

"I was going to say," persisted Mrs. Bell, "that we would only put an animal down if it was very very sick. The only thing wrong with Grumps is his timer."

"Life has become very topsy-turvy because of it," said her husband. "Besides, he's old-fashioned. Modern robots can do so much more."

"What more do we need him to do?"

Her family was momentarily thrown by the question.

"Have proper legs and a flexible body so it can play games with us," suggested Gavin. "It could run and kick a ball."

"We should buy one with long tapering fingers that can wash my hair and plait it for me," said Fleur dreamily.

Mrs. Bell looked expectantly at her husband.

"Well, as Gavin says, it would be nice to have one that can play games."

"Very nice," agreed Mrs. Bell, "but not essential." Her voice took on a pleading tone. "Grumps has served us loyally over the years. It really doesn't matter to me whether he's animal, vegetable or mineral, or not. What does it say about us if we send an otherwise good robot to the scrapheap just because he isn't perfect?"

Her husband and children looked at each other, tacitly agreeing that it was useless to argue. Each had a point of view, but none of them felt as strongly as Mrs. Bell.

"It still doesn't solve our problem," said Mr. Bell.

"Why don't we keep Grumps and buy a new robot to help him?" said Gavin.

His mum seemed lost in thought.

"That's a good idea," said his dad. "Mind you, two robots, two adults and three children . . . it could be a bit crowded."

"Can I leave the table?" said Fleur. "I have to get on with my project."

Mrs. Bell suddenly became animated. "We'd need one that could fit in with Grumps if they're going to work together. Peter, why don't you ask your friend, the professor, for advice?"

Fleur turned back at the door. "I've got a good suggestion. My friend Marcia's just bought the latest model. It's called a BDC4 and it's—"

"Far beyond our means." Her dad rolled his eyes. "The only people who can afford something that sophisticated are technocrats or government ministers. Your friend Marcia is in a different league from us. Honestly, when you think what complex machinery that girl has just to carry her bags . . . I hadn't thought of the professor, Chloe. I'll call him today."

"Huh!" cried Fleur, as she flounced out of the room. "What does a professor know about style?"

Shortly after, Mr. Bell left for his meeting and Gavin played with Charlotte until Grumps had cleared away the breakfast things.

"I'm interviewing over the gobey for an hour or so," said Mrs. Bell, who was in charge of employment (human and robotic) at a large hotel. "Then I'm going into work and taking

19

Charlotte to the day care center. You're staying at home, aren't you?"

"Till this afternoon," said Gavin, and waited for her to disappear before bounding to the top of the house. Passing the study area, he noticed that Fleur was already working on the gobetween. He had plenty to do himself but first he had some burning questions to ask.

Underneath the roof was an entire room devoted to the gobetween. Gavin went in and selected a pair of glasses from a hook on the wall. He slipped them on and stood in front of the large screen.

"Get me Socrates," he said.

There appeared a middle-aged man with a protruding stomach, sitting beneath an olive tree. He wore the homespun white robe of the ancient Greeks. Gavin sat on the grass opposite him.

"Socrates, do you think a robot has rights?"

Socrates frowned. "I am not familiar with the term you use. What is a robot?"

Of course, they had no such thing in 420 BC, although Gavin would not have been surprised if they had invented the notion. Unfortunately he couldn't think of another word that the Greek might know.

"It's a machine that can think. Some of them aren't that clever and just do a particular job like building walls, but some of them are very intelligent and are a bit like us."

The philosopher leaned back against the tree. "And why should this machine have rights?"

"That's what I'm wondering," said Gavin. "You and I talked the other day about animals having rights, and I thought about it and they do."

Socrates nodded but it was hard to tell if he approved. Gavin knew from experience that he didn't say what he thought. He simply asked lots of questions until you saw the answer for yourself.

Gavin went on, "Then you asked whether humans had a right to be free—I knew my answer to that one because we don't believe in slavery nowadays. Then you said what about a right to be happy. I'm not sure about that, but if we do, I don't see why robots shouldn't be happy too."

"And what would make a robot happy?"

"Dad says it's making humans happy because that's what they're programmed . . . built to do."

"What about free will?" asked Socrates. "Does the robot have any freedom to choose how it behaves?"

Gavin hesitated. "Not if it can only do what we tell it to do, I suppose. But then, if we built a robot that could choose for itself . . ."—after many sessions with the philosopher he had grown used to reflecting on his own questions—"then it *would* have free will. So then we should give it the right to choose to be happy, or free, or whatever. Otherwise, it would be wrong to build it with free will," he concluded.

He was very pleased with his logic but Socrates looked agitated. It was obviously difficult for him, not knowing what a robot was.

"Why don't you think about it overnight?" Gavin suggested, which was a way of telling the programmers that Socrates needed more information to be able to help.

Generally at this point a sign would appear saying ASK PLATO or HOBBES, and Gavin would call up another philosopher. Today there was nothing. He decided to leave Socrates onscreen in case he learnt a bit more by tomorrow.

CHAPTER 3

"Do you really think Mum and Dad will buy a new robot?" Fleur whispered to Gavin. They were walking to the learning center later in the day. Grumps was a few steps behind them, concentrating all his faculties on watching for dangers.

"Fancy getting so upset over a machine," she went on. "If only they'd buy one like Marcie's. I haven't seen her yet, but Marcie says this BDC4 is unlike any robot she's ever had."

They turned a corner and found the way blocked by roadworks. Dozens of robotinas were mending potholes in the pavement. They scuttled around like giant beetles, dragging stones and digging holes with their outsize arms. Usually Gavin enjoyed watching their frenetic activity, but today he hurried by. He had a funny feeling in the pit of his stomach. It might have been the soup, but he didn't think so.

Fleur fell silent, imagining herself escorted by a tall bronzed robot with long curvy limbs. His burnished metal gleamed in the sunlight so that people stopped to gape at him. Then they turned to look at Fleur, as if wondering who she could be to have such a regal companion. Fleur ignored the stares, her head held high, like a technobrat accustomed to curiosity and admiration. Crowds began to gather but she and the robot strolled nonchalantly on. The people parted to let them pass—

"If I may say so, Miss Fleur"—Grumps' voice interrupted her reverie—"you appear very distracted."

"I was busy thinking!" said Fleur. "Honestly, you're so grumpy, no wonder we call you Grumps."

"I am sorry if I have annoyed you. I am worried about your crossing the road. The traffic is very busy at this hour."

Fleur realized that they had come to the main road, which separated the residential area from the factories and offices. The learning center was just beyond. Pods whizzed along in both directions, bearing deliveries and supplies, their polished titanium shells as bright as silver. Some of the larger ones carried building materials, furniture or robot workers.

As the children approached the crossing, it emitted a signal to stop the traffic. The pods came to a halt. The Bells were about to cross when an enormous lorry sped by, ignoring the red light that belatedly lit up. Grumps automatically stepped forward, shielding the children and forcing them back onto the pavement. The lorry was followed by another and another: an entire convoy thundered along the road. Gavin whistled in amazement.

"They were petrol-powered; there must be new supplies."

Fleur wasn't interested in petrol. It was smelly and the fumes made you cough. They crossed the road. Behind them, the pods whirred into action once more. "Well," she persisted, "what do you think? Will they buy a new robot?"

"I expect so," said Gavin. "But nothing exciting. We'll probably get one of those new monks—the ones that speak softly and serve food on bamboo trays. Mum will say it'll be good for Charlotte—it'll teach her to be enlightened, or something."

They had reached the entrance to the learning center, a wide stone gateway with human figures and robots carved in relief. A plaque on one of the posts read: CENTER FOR LIFE-LONG LEARNING AND ACHIEVEMENT. Inside, people of all ages were purposefully crisscrossing the courtyard. A group came into sight from the direction of the art block. One of them, an oddly glowing figure, was towered over by a golden robot.

"I believe that is your friend Marcia, Miss Fleur," observed Grumps.

"Yes. You can go now," said Fleur hastily. She dreaded Marcia making fun of Grumps in public, which she often did.

"I am sorry, Miss Fleur," said Grumps. "I would not be fulfilling my duty were I not to escort you to the door."

It was too late. Marcia came around the corner just as they reached the bottom of the steps to the main building. Her golden companion was the robot of Fleur's dreams: her head a burnished dome; her long limbs sculpted like the statue of a Greek goddess. The BDC4 robot was far more beautiful in real life than in the advertisements on the gobetween. Fleur noted with envy that the light glinted off her metal, although it was not a particularly sunny day.

"Yoohoo!" called Marcia. She walked up to them and locked arms with Fleur. "Hi, Fleur. Hello, Gavin. Meet our new machine," she said offhandedly. "We've decided to call her Boadicea."

A few other children had gathered round, though Marcia affected not to notice them.

"I'm so hot!" she confided to Fleur in a loud voice. "I really should set Boadicea at a slower pace, but she looks so elegant when she strides along."

Fleur and Gavin stared at Marcia's dress, which had been glowing a faint orange beneath her coat. Before their eyes it was gradually turning a cool blue. "That's better," said Marcia, tucking a long strand of chestnut-colored hair behind her ear. She was used to people staring at her clothes, many of which changed color in response to variations in her body heat. Once she had shown Fleur a party dress that went through all the hues of the rainbow, causing her to shimmer in a thousand lights.

"Boadicea, say hello to Fleur and Gavin."

The robot looked the children up and down. "Hi," she said. "I've just spent the morning watching Marcie in the art room. She's so talented, don't you think?"

She spoke in a lazy drawl like someone used to lying beside a pool in a hot climate. Yet her eyes were lively and her metal lips parted in a fetching smile.

Neither Gavin nor Fleur knew how to respond. They were not used to robots asking their opinion.

"I've just biscuit-fired my pot," Marcia told Fleur. "I'm going home to research Byzantine pottery to get some ideas for decorating it. You haven't forgotten you're coming round this evening?"

"No," said Fleur.

"Come along, Boadicea." Marcia summoned her with an imperious wave of her hand. "You really should get a new robot, Fleur. Grumps is a joke. Byeee!"

Gavin was surprised that Fleur didn't respond to Marcia. "Bye, Grumps," he said. "I'll call you when I want you to collect me." He waited until Grumps had moved off before asking his sister, "Why didn't you tell Marcia we're getting a new robot?"

"What's the point? We'll never compete with Boadicea."

Fleur and Gavin climbed the steps to the main building, an immense stone structure with Greek columns at the entrance. Big glass doors parted to let them enter. As they walked across the marbled hallway there was a discreet chirping from the jinn on Gavin's wrist. "Gavin, your dad is calling."

A bell-like sound joined in. "It's your father, Fleur!"

Fleur also wore her jinn on her wrist. "Not now," she told it. "Can't stop, Gavin, it's interactive maths. Let me know what Dad says. See you later." And she ran off down the corridor.

Gavin decided to talk to his dad on a bigger screen. "Transfer message to nearest gobey," he told the jinn, hurrying toward a cubicle by the entrance.

"Gavin Bell. There's a message for me," he said as he entered.

"Confirmed," said the cubicle.

A gobetween filled the width of the far wall. Gavin's father was on the screen, standing in a palatial room. Behind him was a holographic model of a low building. Several men and women, many of them dressed in identical red-and-gray suits, were milling around, chatting to each other or examining the model.

With a jolt, Gavin realized that he must be looking at some of the most important people on the planet—the directors of LifeCorp. They ran the company that provided transport, food, water, learning centers, factories, houses and almost everything else he could think of. He couldn't resist staring at them. They were of different nationalities but, apart from the suits, appeared just like everyone else. He wasn't sure what he would have expected.

Mr. Bell stood with his back to the gobetween, talking to a gray-haired man who looked Chinese. The man wore small wire-rimmed glasses—most people had their sight corrected by laser or through gene therapy at conception. The glasses gave him a slightly bemused look. He too wore the red-and-gray suit.

"Hello, Dad."

Mr. Bell turned round. "Hello, Gavin. Excuse me," he addressed the Chinese-looking man, who instead of walking away moved closer to the screen.

"So this is your son." He peered at Gavin. "Your father is very intelligent. Very fine architect. This factory will be one of the best in the world. You know, we are going to build the next generation of BDCs."

Gavin glowed with pride. His father raised an eyebrow in modesty.

The man continued, "Let me tell you something. These BDC4s are unlike any robot you have ever seen. Just you wait." He grinned.

Gavin guessed that the man would be disappointed if he told him he had met a BDC4 only a moment ago, so he nodded.

"See you," said the man with a wave of his hand. He moved toward the group around the model.

"Just a quick call," said Gavin's dad. "As you can tell, we're about to begin the presentation to the corporation. I called my friend, Professor Ogden, to ask his advice. He was very excited when I told him of our decision. He wouldn't say why. . . ."

Over his father's shoulder, Gavin could still see the man with the spectacles, who stiffened and looked back at Mr. Bell. Gavin had an impulse to interrupt his father. He moved close to the screen and spoke quietly. "Euphoric, Dad. I've . . . er . . . got to wing, though."

"I'm going to visit him after this meeting. Your mum's working but I thought you and Fleur would like to come. I can pick you up at five."

"Fleur's going to see Marcia. But I can come."

"Good," said his dad. "I don't know why you're whispering. . . ."

The man had moved further away but might still be in earshot. Gavin was uneasy, although he did not know why.

"I'd better go," said his dad. "See you later."

Gavin told the gobetween to switch itself off. He felt foolish. Of course the LifeCorp man had not been interested in their conversation. Probably, he had reacted to what someone at the table had said, or perhaps he had remembered something important. He certainly looked a bit annoyed, as if he'd left something behind in his hotel room, for instance. Anyway, what did it matter if he had overheard them?

Yet an uncertainty was nagging at Gavin.

He left the cubicle and continued along the corridor toward the changing rooms. His game of liveball would be starting in ten minutes. He remembered to contact Fleur on her jinn. She didn't answer—no doubt she was in the middle of an experiment—so he left her a message to tell her he was going later to see the professor. He sent the same message home to Grumps.

Gavin changed quickly and joined the other liveballers on the playing field. A thin drizzle of rain had started to fall; already the ground was slippery.

"Let's go!" shouted the coach, and the warm-up began. The ball was set to rise at a low height but still it led the players an exhausting dance as it swooped and zigzagged past them. Suddenly, it was heading straight for Gavin's chest. He ran forward to catch it and the ball veered away. Gavin dived after it, missed and fell into the mud.

"You moonrock!" cried his friend Omar as he ran past.

Gavin was about to get up when an image flashed into his mind. He saw again the man from LifeCorp walking away from his father, then abruptly stopping and glancing back at him. It had happened so quickly that Gavin had not registered it at the time, but now he was sure he was not mistaken. The man had looked round at the precise moment his father had mentioned Professor Ogden. And the expression on his face had not been friendly.

For the rest of the game, Gavin was so distracted that he spent most of it on the ground. The final whistle blew and he realized that he would have to rush if he was going to get all the mud off in time to meet his dad.

"Are you all right?" asked Omar, breaking off from congratulating the winners. "I've never seen you play so badly. Like a first-generation robot."

"Sorry," breathed Gavin, "got to wing."

Mr. Bell was waiting at the other side of the hallway. He waved. Gavin ran toward him, skidding the last few meters of the polished floor.

"No need to hurry," said Mr. Bell.

The big glass doors refused to open. Two women, arriving at the top of the steps and finding their way blocked, frowned in exasperation. Mr. Bell shrugged apologetically. A thin tubular robot with no arms or legs slithered over to him.

"Excuse me." Its optic sensors swiveled round to examine Mr. Bell's face. "We do not recognize you as authorized to accompany this boy."

Mr. Bell stroked his chin. "I've just had a haircut—perhaps that's the problem. I fancy it gives me a squarer jaw, a bit more 'all action hero.'" He winked at Gavin, who smiled back, but the robot was not amused.

"I shall have to take a retinogram. If you would lean forward . . ."

The robot's optic sensors fixed on Mr. Bell's eyes. He tried not to blink. "Bell, Peter," said the robot. "Father of Fleur and Gavin."

"That's me," said Mr. Bell cheerfully.

"Thank you, Mr. Bell." The glass doors opened. "Have a good evening. Goodbye, Gavin."

CHAPTER 4

"**We have to take the** hoverbus," said Mr. Bell. "There's one along in a moment."

Daylight was fading. Though the rain had stopped, the pavements were wet and shiny under the streetlamps.

"Dad, who's that Chinese man?" said Gavin as they turned the corner from the learning center. "You know, the one I met on the gobey."

"Chinese? Ah, you mean Mr. Lobsang. He's Tibetan, not Chinese. He's one of LifeCorp's top robot designers."

"He tried to listen to our conversation—I think it was because you mentioned Professor Ogden."

"Really? Perhaps they've met. They're in the same field, after all," said Mr. Bell.

"He looked funny," said Gavin.

"Funny?"

"As if he'd like to run the professor over, given half the chance."

"Hmm," responded Mr. Bell. "Well, scientists don't always see eye to eye."

They heard the drone of the hoverbus. Mr. Bell held out his jinn and the hoverbus homed in, swooping low to the level of the pavement. The curved double doors parted. His dad climbed on but the step up was too high for Gavin. The hoverbus realized its mistake and sank closer to the curb.

"Welcome aboard," said the conductor. She extended her thin metal fingers to scan their travel passes, then stepped aside to let them into the body of the bus.

The hoverbus was half full of people who looked as if they had important business in town. Gavin counted at least ten suits and spotted several very expensive jinns. A monitor on a screen showed the path that the hoverbus was taking. Mr. Bell spoke the name of the street they were visiting.

"Sorry, that street is too far from our route. Please select another destination or alight at the nearest stop indicated by the red light."

"Looks like we'll have a bit of a walk, but it isn't too far," said Mr. Bell.

Gavin loved the hoverbus and wished he could travel on it more often. You could watch a movie on the small screen in front of you, or listen to music, or pick up a lexiscreen to read the news or a story. But he preferred to size up the robots on board. He nudged his father. "Look at that one. I bet it could crush this bus between its hands if it wanted to."

His dad turned to look at the robot in question. It was over two meters high and very broad. "Too big for us," he said.

"That one belongs on a building site. Can you imagine it making tea or changing Charlotte's nappy?"

Tea making had not been part of Gavin's fantasy. He had been imagining exactly what people at the learning center would say to him, with a robot built like a colossus. No one would ever try to bully you if you had one of those.

At the front of the bus a message continuously scrolled across a wide screen. Gavin waited for the beginning of the text and read:

Welcome aboard the *Argos*. Your conductor for today is Dora. Patrons are kindly requested to observe the following:

- to be furnished with a valid pass for their journey.
- to address each other with respect and consideration at all times.
- to converse in modulated tones.
- to refrain from eating or drinking (refreshments may be purchased and consumed at any of our termini. Please ask Dora for menus).
- to sit wherever possible. There is standing room for 20 entities.
- standing patrons to hold on to a pole at all times in case of turbulence or an emergency stop.

LifeCorp reserves the right to eject from the hoverbus any such entities who do not comply with the above. Thank you for traveling on the corporation hoverbus the *Argos*.

▪ ▪ ▪ ▪ ▪

Next to the screen was a graphic of a person with multiple heads, to indicate that the message was available in numerous languages. Gavin idly wondered whether the computer knew ancient Greek but decided to find out another time. The hoverbus had risen almost to roof level and the lure of looking in people's windows before the blinds came down was hard to resist.

A series of domestic snapshots flickered by him: a woman walking upstairs with a work case and several misshapen carrier bags; a grandmother placing bowls of food before two small children; an older boy stirring a pot while his father chopped vegetables on a wooden board; all of them scarcely noticing a second shadowy world played out behind them in the eerie glow of the gobetween.

His dad followed his gaze. "Not jealous, are you? Of the gobey in every room?"

Gavin shook his head. "It's not as if we can't use it when we want."

"And there's always the middle of the night," joked Mr. Bell.

"The house spies on me!" Gavin blurted out.

"What?"

"It threatens to tell Mum if I don't go back to bed. She told it to."

"How long before it stops you?"

Gavin did not want to lie. "Half an hour, maybe," he admitted.

"Then that's not spying." His dad sounded relieved. "That's keeping a friendly eye on you, like a grandparent would."

"S'pose so," said Gavin. Mr. Bell put down the lexiscreen he had been reading.

"You know, your mum and I discussed this when we built the house. We agreed it would be dreadful to spy on our own children. You've a right to privacy like anyone else. That's why we don't ask Grumps questions. His job is to protect you—to be a guardian, not a guard." Mr. Bell smiled, as if pleased with his turn of phrase.

Gavin could think of several of his friends whose parents did spy on them. They were constantly inventing ways to distract their house or robot. "Thanks, Dad. I suppose it means you trust us."

He looked out of the window again. It was almost dusk and a steady stream of hoverbuses and flying pods was leaving the city. Hundreds of white lights danced toward them like smiling faces. Then the bus was skirting buildings again, and he realized with a shiver of excitement and apprehension that they had entered the city center.

The buildings were taller here and seemed to form one crowded unbroken row. Thrusting metal structures and concrete monoliths overshadowed ancient buildings of brick and stone. All they had in common was a grimy façade. It was as if the city had been in suspended animation for many years, unable to build anything new, not even able to decay.

Gavin's father once told him that many of the buildings had

been office blocks. Now their shuttered windows represented thousands of dwellings, one on top of the other. The shutters gave the impression that the inhabitants had shut themselves away from life. Gavin knew this was fanciful, that during the day the streets were teeming with people. Even now, if he craned his neck to look down as far as possible, he could see them heading into bars and gobey halls.

Yet who could tell what went on behind closed windows? Gavin tried to imagine what life in the city would be like. Most city people did not have jobs since labor had been taken over by robots. They lived in the city to be fed and entertained. It might be a friendly place to live, he told himself, remembering the row upon row of hedges in Wynston Avenue.

Sudden bursts of bright light interrupted the orange glow of the streetlamps. For a long stretch of the route, every spare centimeter of building was covered with a flashing parade of virtual robots. No wonder people hid behind shutters, thought Gavin, when the front of their house was a billscreen.

"There's a BDC4!" he cried. "Oh, you missed it." He managed to make out the slogan: "Robot by name, friend by nature."

Gavin watched the displays for a moment longer. A thought struck him. "Dad, why do they bother to advertise these robots in the city? If professionals like you and Mum can't afford them, there's no way the city people can."

His father hesitated. "Propaganda," he said at last.

"What's that?"

Mr. Bell rubbed his chin. "It's a message to the rest of us that the technocrats have the most powerful robots."

"But that's like saying . . ." Gavin broke off. He wondered why he'd never realized it before now. "That's like saying the technocrats are somehow better than the rest of us."

His dad laughed, unconvincingly, it sounded to Gavin. They fell silent.

The hoverbus dipped toward a park, full of trees, where an elderly lady and her small dog were waiting. Dora stepped down, picked up the dog in one hand and with the other steadied the woman by the elbow. The doors were closing behind them when two young men dived through the gap. Without glancing at Dora, they held out their passes to be scanned and ran to the center of the bus, where they started to climb up the poles, monkey style. The shorter of the two leant over and snatched the other's woolly hat.

Dora marched down the aisle. "This behavior is not acceptable. Please sit down."

"We're holding on to the poles, aren't we? What's your problem?" said the man who had grabbed the hat.

"This is not an acceptable way of holding on to the poles. LifeCorp will not be responsible for any injury—"

Before she could finish, the man stretched out an arm and thrust the hat over her face. There was a gasp from one of the people in suits. Gavin grinned and turned to his dad. He was startled to see Mr. Bell's tight-lipped expression.

Although Dora had lost her sight momentarily, her sensors

told her the exact position of her attacker. She stepped forward, seized the young man by the shoulders and plucked him from the pole, which he made a futile attempt to cling to with his legs. Swinging him across the aisle, she put him gently on a seat, as if he was the final cherry on a cake.

His companion quickly jumped down and sat beside him, trying to look nonchalant. The first man folded his arms and glared out of the window.

"Dora showed them," laughed Gavin.

"Silly to mess with machines," muttered his dad.

Gavin frowned. "A robot won't ever harm a human, will it? That's the way they're programmed."

"You're right," said Mr. Bell. "But as you've just seen, in a show of force a robot will win. I learnt that to my cost when I was younger."

"What do you mean?" asked Gavin excitedly. It was novel to imagine his dad as some sort of gladiator, facing a snarling-jawed robot on the battlefield.

A red light appeared on the monitor. "Some other time," said Mr. Bell. "This is our stop."

CHAPTER 5

Marcia lived in the technocrats' quarter a kilometer or two from the learning center. This was one of the few journeys Fleur was allowed to make unaccompanied.

Most of the route was under surveillance by cameras and robot patrols, but sometimes Mrs. Bell was nervous about the short distance, especially if there had been a message on the gobetween to say marauders were about. Though one day Fleur had overheard her remark to Mr. Bell that she didn't always believe the messages. "Sometimes I think they just want to keep us off the streets," her mum had said.

It was intoxicating to walk on her own, to have a sense that she might choose to do whatever she wanted, even if all she did was visit Marcia. Fleur felt lighter, yet confident and strong, as if her presence was somehow outlined in bold ink. She was more aware than usual of her surroundings, of the gradually darkening sky and the drip drip of raindrops from the trees along the pavement.

She wondered what awaited her. Marcia's family led a

chaotic life and every time Fleur visited, there was a commotion of some sort.

The security gate had been primed to expect Fleur and recognized her from the data in its bank. When it told her it was safe to do so, she walked through the hot fence that guarded the entrance and went uphill to the Morrises' house. From the outside it looked deceptively quiet. She went up to the front door.

"Fleur Bell," the house identified her. "You may enter." The door slid to one side and Fleur stepped into the hall. Or what used to be the hall. Today it was much narrower, like a bowling alley, and appeared to stretch the length of the building. There seemed to be no doors in the new hall so Fleur had no choice but to wait until someone appeared. Judging by the noise, there were several people in the house. Gunshots reverberated from a room next to her, while on the other side of the opposite wall a cheerful male voice was saying, "To the right! To the left! And up and up and up!" She also thought she could hear the faint strains of a stringed instrument.

She had just decided to walk down the narrow hall and try to find the stairs that led to Marcia's room when a wall moved across in front of her, blocking her way. At first she was startled; then she saw that the wall completely filled the gap from ceiling to floor. She recalled how suddenly and smoothly it had slid into place and her surprise turned to alarm.

Hastily she made for the front door. But no sooner had she turned on her heels than a second wall appeared, blocking the way again. She was trapped. There were no doors or windows in the high box that now enclosed her, nor could she see any control buttons or voice-activated panels on the walls. The sounds of gunshots were closer now and drowned out the other noises, if indeed they were still being made.

Fleur wondered how loudly she would have to shout to be heard. Then, out of the corner of her eye, she sensed something moving. She didn't dare look. Other than her there was nothing else in the box. Breathing rapidly, she steeled herself to peer sideways. Slowly but perceptibly the wall was closing inward.

"Heeelp!" It was more of a scream than a cry. Fleur strained her ears to hear if there was a response above the din next door. She called again. *"Help!"* The shooting noises died down slightly and this time Fleur thought she could hear voices. She banged on the wall and cried: "Let me out! Don't squash me! Please don't squash me!"

Everything went quiet. "Fleur, is that you?" asked a thin anxious voice.

"Yes," said Fleur, trying to keep her voice steady. To her immense relief all four walls moved away and one of them slid back to reveal Marcia, her brother, BJ, and their parents, gathered together in the Morrises' living room.

"Bit of a close shave, that," grunted Marcia's father.

"I can't understand how it could happen," declared her mother. "The walls aren't supposed to move of their own accord. At least, there's nothing in the instructions. Are you sure you didn't press anything?"

Fleur was trembling with shock. She longed to retort that there had been nothing to press and that that had been part of the problem, but she didn't trust herself to speak. She tried not to look at Marcia's brother, who was glaring furiously at her.

"Dad spent all afternoon rearranging the rooms," said Marcia accusingly. "We didn't know you were here."

"The house let me in," muttered Fleur, hoping she didn't sound as scared as she felt. Though part of her thought she had every right to be scared and would have liked the Morrises to acknowledge this.

"The house did say something . . . ," said Marcia's mother. "We couldn't hear it properly. BJ was taking part in the Charge of the Light Brigade. He was about to lead an attack on the Russians' left flank."

Fleur didn't have a clue what Mrs. Morris was talking about, but she said "Oh" as if she understood. The Morris family continued to stand in a huddle, staring at her. She made a big effort and said, as airily as she could, "Was something wrong with the house? Is that why you moved the walls?"

The Morrises looked at each other, astonished. "We fancied a change," said Marcia's mother.

"Variety is the spice of life," said Mr. Morris. "And technology's the mill that grinds it to your taste." He smiled for the first time.

"Oh," said Fleur again.

Marcia stepped forward. "You look a bit pale," she said.

"Let's go upstairs." She led Fleur through what was now the living room.

"Come back, Mrs. Morris, you haven't finished your abdominals!" cried a lively voice.

Fleur glanced round at the speaker and couldn't see anyone.

"That's Ramirez, Mum's virtual fitness trainer," whispered Marcia. "Mum's fallen in love with him."

Fleur giggled, despite still feeling shocked.

"But it's hopeless since he isn't real," went on Marcia, "so she's bought Dad a leotard instead."

The image of Mr. Morris in a leotard was too much for Fleur. She burst out laughing. Marcia looked pleased. "And when Mum does well in her exercises, as a reward Ramirez plays the guitar and sings to her and now she wants Dad—"

"That's enough!" cried Fleur, but Marcia was also laughing and couldn't go on.

The door at the far end of the living room opened and the sound of a haunting melody was unmistakable. They went through the door and came out where the stairs now were. Fleur jumped. A young woman she had never seen before was playing the violin, her eyes half closed in concentration. "Hologram," said Marcia matter-of-factly. "Dad likes it."

Fleur mutely followed Marcia up the stairs. She was used to the Morrises' obsession with technology. The house was full of it and each time she visited they were trying something new. Usually she was excited to discover the latest gadget even if, sometimes, it was not very successful. But today had been particularly chaotic, dangerous even. She felt sick as she recalled the moving walls.

"You're lucky the walls weren't soundproofed," Marcia remarked. "Some of them are, but since Dad's rearranged them we don't know which ones." The lurching feeling in Fleur's stomach grew worse.

Marcia turned on the stairs and faced her. "You don't really think you'd have been killed, do you?" She didn't wait for Fleur to answer. "The walls are designed to stop the moment they bump into something. No one would buy them if they squashed people's favorite furniture or crushed their pets to death, would they?"

Fleur felt a surge of anger. Marcia was making it sound as if it was all her fault. "How was I supposed to know?" she demanded.

Marcia continued up the stairs. "You're not used to modern technology," she said mildly. "The technology in your house is antique. After all, your mum reads books!"

Fleur also read books, but she didn't say so. She liked the feel of them, their compactness, the smoothness of the cover and the grainy texture of the paper that, she fancied, had a woody, dusty smell, reminiscent of the outside. She enjoyed having to turn the page, and the anticipation of the ending as the remaining pages grew fewer.

If you really hate books, why do you spend so many hours

sketching in them? thought Fleur. But, as often happens, it was too late to make the retort.

They had crossed the landing to Marcia's bedroom. As the door opened, Fleur could see that the walls were bathed in a shimmering blue light. They walked in. The entire room was flooded in the light. In places it was so dense as to be inky blue; in others it was a clear turquoise.

"It's like being underwater!" cried Fleur.

"Here," said Marcia, handing her a simulsuit. Fleur wriggled her toes into the feet of the suit and pulled it up over her body. There were gloves at the end of the arms and it took her a while to fit her fingers into the right holes. The padded suit made her fingers thick and clumsy and it was difficult to fasten the zip.

"Hurry up," urged Marcia, who was already in her suit and about to slip on a helmet. Fleur put on a helmet too and the world changed. They were underwater. The inky patches grew darker, the bedroom walls receded and the turquoise, blue, and black seemed to go on forever. Scores of tiny bubbles appeared on the outside of the helmet as if Fleur was breathing with an air cylinder.

Gingerly, she stepped forward and felt the resistance of an entire ocean against her body. Although she knew she was walking on the floor, the pads on the soles of the suit gave her the sensation of buoyancy. Soon she forgot about the carpet beneath her feet and instinctively began to use her arms to propel herself forward.

As she grew used to the haziness of the water and the occasional darkness she noticed objects on the ocean bed—rocks, barnacles, an upturned boat. Something tapped her on the shoulder. It was Marcia, beckoning her to follow. They dived further into the nocturnal depths.

CHAPTER 6

Gavin was astonished to find himself still in the heart of the city. He had expected Professor Ogden to work in a laboratory on an industrial estate. His father noticed his surprise. "He works from home. You don't need that much space in his line of work. It's like architecture—we create large buildings from inside small offices."

"What exactly does Professor Ogden do?" said Gavin as they walked along. He had not thought to ask before and realized that he had only a vague idea of some kind of scientist.

From the time it took him to reply, Mr. Bell was not a lot clearer in his own mind. "He's an inventor, I'd say. A designer. I met him when he came to advise us about an intelligent building we were having problems with. It turned out not to be very intelligent. It kept letting everyone into the house except the owners. Professor Ogden devised a solution. But he doesn't talk much about his work."

Mr. Bell was leading them down a warren of narrow streets. To Gavin's surprise, passersby nodded and smiled at them.

This was certainly friendlier than Wynston Avenue. All the same, he couldn't help casting anxious looks around him in case a marauder should be lurking.

The buildings were even older than the ones they had passed on the bus, but much less high. At last Mr. Bell stopped in front of a whitewashed brick house that would have looked more at home in the countryside.

"Good evening, Mr. Bell; good evening, Gavin," said a disembodied voice.

Gavin jumped. It was such an old-fashioned house that he hadn't expected any new technology. He climbed to the top step and peered at the door. The door opened and he found himself virtually nose to chest with a stocky man. His father stepped forward and shook the man's hand. "Hello, Professor."

"Good to see you again, Peter," said the professor. He offered his hand to Gavin, who took it a little awkwardly.

"How did the door see us?"

The professor smiled. "Technology," he said. "Or, if you prefer, magic. It's all the same." He ushered them in and took their coats. Gavin tried not to stare. Although he did not seem particularly old, the professor's thick head of hair was completely white. Through an open door Gavin spotted a neat, carpeted sitting room. Professor Ogden noticed his disappointment.

"Shall we go straight up to the lab?"

He briskly led them up two flights of stairs to the top of the house. Undetectably, the atmosphere changed. It was as if they had climbed to a great height—the top of an alpine mountain, for instance. Gavin and his father instinctively drew deep breaths to fill their lungs with clear fresh air. The professor watched them.

A panel in the wall slid open and the laboratory was revealed. It was a large room that ran the width of the house. The far wall was a series of tall windows and at one end of the room were rows of computers. Four or five robots of a type Gavin did not recognize sat in front of the screens.

The other end of the room was half hidden by a large whiteboard. A group of people stood beside it, using their hands to move images around and write symbols. Those who glanced at Gavin and his father as they entered quickly turned back to their work.

The professor invited them to sit down at a round table in the corner, then excused himself for a moment. A robot appeared with a tray of tea, biscuits, and a soft drink for Gavin.

Looking about him, Gavin felt dejected. In his view an inventor's laboratory should be exciting and dynamic, a fairground of fast-moving graphics and simulations, where designers whispered top-secret ideas to one another. The resemblance to his father's office was not at all what he had expected. Nor were tea and biscuits.

As he gazed around the room he caught a movement in the corner of his eye. He turned his head and the object came into view. It was a luminous ball, floating in the air. He watched as it wafted across the room. No one else seemed to have noticed it. His father was pouring himself a cup of tea and Gavin was too stunned to call to him.

In a flash, the ball's light passed beyond its perimeter, like the rays of a miniature sun. The next moment its edge was clearly defined again. Gavin thought the outpouring of light must have been a trick of the light.

The ball approached the table and hovered there for an instant. Mr. Bell, reaching for a biscuit, was oblivious. The workers in the room had their heads down or were deep in conversation with each other. The ball floated on toward the far wall and appeared to sail through a windowpane.

Gavin blinked. He hadn't imagined it—the ball had vanished. But how could it have passed through a sheet of glass? Perhaps he had imagined the ball of light in the first place. No, he had seen it, all right.

"Dad," he began, but at that moment Professor Ogden emerged from behind the whiteboard and joined them at the table.

"I've got a surprise for you!" he said, beaming. "I must confess, I was a little anxious since EGR3 is only a prototype, but now I've tidied up one or two . . . local difficulties, I think we can solve your problem in return for a little, shall we say, ground-level research?"

Even Mr. Bell seemed to find this hard to follow. "Are you saying you might have a robot for us?" he asked.

"Precisely," said the professor. "We have been working on this model for some time. It's a rather groundbreaking experiment, if I might say so. But it's too soon to launch it on the world. Indeed, we shall have to think carefully how we might do that. . . ." A somber look came over his face, and his attention drifted for a second or two.

"No matter," he continued. "That's where you can be of great service. If we can test EGR3 in a safe, friendly environment then we shall know whether it really can do all that we believe it to be capable of."

Mr. Bell still wore a puzzled expression. "I don't quite understand where we fit in. I mean, if this robot is so remarkable, you can't be suggesting it comes to work for us?"

"Why not?" Professor Ogden sounded rather abrupt.

"Don't you think our requirements are a bit . . . modest? Housework, escorting the children . . ."

The professor laughed. "Can you remember what robots were first used for, in the twentieth century?"

"I know," said Gavin. "Working in factories, making cars and fridges, those sorts of things."

"Exactly. All a robot needed to 'know' was how to do its particular task. It had only one thing to do and it stayed in the same place to do it. Do you know how long it took us scientists to build a robot that can see and hear and reason and move around? Decades! Imagine boiling an egg . . ."

Gavin frowned at this new chain of thought. What had boiling an egg got to do with inventing robots?

"It's about the simplest cooking you can do," went on the professor, "but if you stop and think about it, it's actually a complicated task. Judging the amount of water to cover the egg, putting the egg in the pan without breaking it, recognizing if the water has boiled dry, judging when the egg is done, knowing that if you tip the pan to empty the water the egg will fall out as well!"

"When I was little," mused Gavin, "I used to copy Mum and Dad filling a saucepan with water. But I never knew you should turn the tap off, and the water used to overflow and my sleeves always got soaked."

"That's it, exactly!" cried the professor. "But you learnt. Now, most robots have this information put in their database by the manufacturer. It's got easier to do over the years because we've been able to build on the knowledge of previous robots. But the dream has always been to build a robot that could learn, and therefore think, for itself."

He stopped talking as if lost in a world of his own. Gavin and his father exchanged glances and waited. Eventually Mr. Bell prompted him: "And EGR3 . . . ?"

The professor pursed his lips as if concentrating on a difficult problem. "Of course," he said thoughtfully, "I can hardly expect you to take on EGR3 without some idea of its unique properties. However, I must stress that this information is highly confidential."

Gavin was agog. Unlikely as it had seemed, the professor was involved in top-secret work after all.

"Commercially sensitive, I suppose," said Gavin's dad knowingly.

"In a way . . ."

Professor Ogden fell silent and Mr. Bell wondered whether to repeat his question. Before he could speak, the professor said simply: "It knows nothing."

Gavin and his father were taken aback. "Well," began Mr. Bell, struggling to be polite. "Is it quite ready for the outside world in that case?"

His friend chuckled. "It knows nothing in the sense that we have not taught it anything. Unlike other robots, which come programmed with information about the world, EGR 3 began life ignorant, just like a baby. It knows quite a bit now, in fact, but everything it knows it has learnt for itself."

"But I thought you said it hadn't been out in the world?" said Mr. Bell.

"True."

"So how can it have learnt much?"

"As I said, we designed the EGR to be like a newborn baby, a stranger to the world. Then we realized two things. The first is that no baby is completely ignorant. Babies are born with certain abilities—to recognize their mother, to signal when they are hungry or thirsty, for example. They are 'programmed' to crawl and walk, to acquire language, and so on. If the mind of our robot were really a clean slate, would it ever learn anything at all?

"Secondly, even if we programmed it with the early abilities of a baby, it would take years before it was even talking!" The professor was very excited by now and speaking rapidly. "So we cheated somewhat," he went on. "We programmed EGR3 with a child's vocabulary. Then for months we placed it in imaginary situations in which to learn about the world. Although it's been no further than this house it has a good deal of knowledge—about water, rivers and seas, buildings, woods, the danger of falling, of losing its way—"

Gavin interrupted. "You mean it's learnt from simulations?"

"Exactly. And from talking about its experiences to me and my researchers."

"I still don't understand where we fit in," said Mr. Bell.

The professor merely looked down at his feet as if the answer might be written on his shoes. Gavin glanced round at the windows, vaguely hoping the luminous ball might reappear. He noticed that it had become dark outside. They had been discussing robots for a long time. At last Professor Ogden looked up.

"EGR3 knows enough to ensure its survival in the physical world. But what it knows at present is a drop in the ocean compared with what it has the potential to know. Besides . . ." He broke off again. Gavin was growing exasperated. What was it that was so important and yet so difficult for the professor to say?

Professor Ogden stood up and moved away from the table. When next he spoke his voice was soft and low, as if he were talking to himself. "We can teach it about the physical world, but we can't teach it about life."

Mr. Bell cleared his throat. "I'm not sure what you mean."

The professor turned to him and smiled almost sadly. "Love, loyalty, kindness, joy, compassion, courage, fear, envy, anger, loss . . ."

"Feelings?"

"But robots don't have feelings, do they, Dad?"

Gavin's father shrugged and looked uncomfortable. The professor continued as if he hadn't heard them. "You can't teach those things in computer simulations."

"You want us to teach—" began Mr. Bell.

Professor Ogden said, "I am not asking you to be its teachers. I am asking you to be its family. EGR3 will learn right and wrong just as your children are learning."

Gavin could tell by his dad's face that he was at a loss what to do. He looked as if someone had offered him a fortune and wanted him to eat a rattlesnake in return. Gavin wondered what was the big dilemma. There were many questions that he was longing to ask and he found himself crying out, "But what exactly can it do?"

His father looked at him in surprise. "Gavin . . . ," he admonished.

"No, no, it's a good question," said the professor. "Here I am, asking you to help raise a robot, and yet you came to me in the first place to ask for help." He laughed. "It struck me as a most fortuitous coincidence. Most fortuitous. You see, EGR3 really can't be left to its own devices. The moment your father explained that you wanted an assistant for—what's his name?

Grumps—I realized this could be the answer to our problem. It sounds to me as if Grumps is actually very able, apart from his timing problem. He just needs a bit of help, as you say. EGR3 will make an ideal assistant."

He noticed Gavin's crestfallen face. "Still waiting for an answer to your question? Tell me first, young man," he said kindly, "what can *you* do?"

"I . . . I don't know, at least, I know some things, that is . . . ," stammered Gavin.

"I'm sure you can do many things. But you know, you are still growing up. Well, I would say the same thing about EGR3. We must wait and see. Wait and see."

While he was speaking the professor had moved closer to the board. He put his head round and beckoned. A figure appeared.

Gavin and his father gasped. For a moment it looked as if a carefully arranged pile of narrow rubber tires were walking toward them. Then they identified a face that had wide rubbery lips, a nub of a nose and round eyes looking somewhat startled.

Professor Ogden was beaming. He placed his hands on the shoulders of the new arrival and announced in an unexpectedly tremulous voice: "Let me introduce you to EGR3."

"Can I really come home with you? Are you really going to help me learn about life?" The robot's male voice was warm and surprisingly expressive. "And Professor Ogden says you have another robot. . . . But I'm forgetting my manners." He stretched out a rubbery hand. "How do you do, Mr. Bell? And you must be Gavin." The lips parted in a smile. "I've never met a boy before."

* * * * *

A short time later they were standing on the steps outside the professor's house, saying goodbye.

"Is there anything else we need to know?" said Mr. Bell nervously.

"I don't think so," said Professor Ogden. "I'll call you in a few weeks to see how things are progressing."

"Can I ask you a question?"

"Of course, Gavin."

"I thought I saw something in your lab, a sort of ball. . . ."

"You did," said the professor carelessly. "Sphere." He made a move to shake Mr. Bell's hand and Gavin understood that the subject was closed.

"Could I just ask one more thing? What happened to EGR1 and 2?"

The professor turned back to Gavin. He looked pleased. "I wondered if you would ask that. Let me see, how to put it in a nutshell? Our first model, EGR1, was very successful at learning. Unfortunately each time it learnt something new, it forgot its previous knowledge! We tried everything to improve its memory, but to no effect. We had to dismantle it." He sighed.

"And EGR2?"

Professor Ogden brightened up. "A great improvement. We learnt from our mistakes and this next prototype could remember everything she learnt. However, that is not necessarily always a good thing. What was worse, she considered every bit of information to be fact. Now, you and I know that cannot be true. If I say it's a lovely day, and you say it's cold and wintry, which is the fact? Yet we are both describing the same day."

"Sounds like she couldn't reason properly," observed Gavin.

"That was part of the problem, yes."

"So did you dismantle her too?" said Mr. Bell.

A shadow passed over the professor's face. "One day we took her for a walk and came to a road. I said the road was clear and we started to cross. Just then my assistant cried out that a convoy was coming. We humans crossed safely or jumped back onto the curb . . ." He broke off.

"And the robot?" urged Gavin.

"Paralysis, I'm afraid. Poor EGR2 was so caught up trying to work out which fact was true—reconciling the two beliefs, as we say—that she couldn't move. Then . . . crushed by a lorry."

It conjured up a horrible picture.

"What a waste," remarked Mr. Bell.

"Not entirely," said the professor with a nod in EGR3's direction. The robot had been waiting patiently at the bottom of the steps. He looked up at his creator with a grateful expression. Professor Ogden smiled affectionately, but briefly.

"Time to go," he said.

CHAPTER 7

Fleur and Marcia had emerged from the ocean floor and were stretched out side by side on Marcia's large bed. They still wore their simulsuits and had the sensation of lying on warm sand. The sun was high above them and they could hear the gentle lapping of waves. Huge butterflies in dazzling colors flitted across the beach.

Fleur turned her face lazily toward Marcia and was disappointed to see that her friend had sat up and was pulling off her helmet. She did likewise and began to unzip her suit.

Wordlessly Marcia left the bed and opened a drawer of her desk. She pulled out a sheet of paper and with surprising care, almost tenderness, laid it on top of the desk. She chose a thick charcoal pencil and began to sketch, covering the paper with swift bold strokes. Fleur didn't dare interrupt. She sat cross-legged and waited.

"You can talk to me," said Marcia. "I can still draw."

"I was just thinking about the beach. Those smells—coconut and lemon and something piney . . . I wonder if it's really like that."

"Simulations are OK but they're nothing like the real thing." Marcia's expression was casual. Fleur looked at her with wide eyes but she carried on sketching as if she hadn't noticed.

"How do you know?" said Fleur. "Have you been there?"

Marcia laughed. "Of course. We all have, lots of times. And not just to beaches. Art galleries, museums, famous buildings, ski slopes . . ."

"But how . . . There's not enough petrol. How did you get there?"

"By plane." She turned round to face Fleur. "You don't know anything, do you? There's still enough good oil around, although it's very expensive to get at it. LifeCorp bought up all the fuel companies and decided to keep it a secret."

"Why?"

"To save the decent petrol for the important people—the government and the technocrats," said Marcia. "We don't want you lot traveling the world, you'll spoil it. Besides, the oil would soon run out. So we only let you have the recycled stuff and that's only good for cars."

"But you're not—"

"Important? Of course I am! I'm the relative of a technocrat. Anything my dad does, we can do too."

"What about the rest of us?" said Fleur dully.

Marcia shrugged. "You get to go on holiday and travel to places. You just can't go far because all you have is recycled petrol." She gave a little shudder as if she could smell the choking fumes. Fleur felt a mixture of anger and bewilderment. Why had her mum and dad never told her this?

"Does everyone else know?"

"Don't be silly!" cried Marcia. "I told you it was a secret." Her face took on a wild expression, and before Fleur knew it she had jumped onto the bed beside her and seized her wrist in both hands. Fleur tried to get free but her friend pulled her arm behind her back, and the harder she struggled the tighter Marcia's grip.

"You mustn't tell anyone," Marcia hissed in her ear. "Promise? It's for your own good. You'll only get into trouble, and so will I." She twisted Fleur's arm further as if to underscore her point. Tears pricked Fleur's eyes. She nodded. Marcia released her arm.

"We'd better go downstairs," she said lightly. "Your tin can will be here soon."

Something fiery welled up in Fleur. She was not going to walk away from Marcia just like that. "As a matter of fact," she declared, "we're buying a new robot. Gavin and my dad are finding out about one this very minute from a world-famous expert. I don't expect we'll have an ordinary robot like Boadicea."

Marcia gaped at her. Fleur stuck out her chin and swept out

of the room and down the stairs. Mrs. Morris was standing at the bottom. "Going so soon?" she said. "Wouldn't you like to stay for supper?"

Fleur always thought her smile was a bit like a robot's—designed to be flashed on and off. "No, thank you," she said, determined not to stay a minute longer in the Morrises' hellish house.

The walk back seemed to take forever. It was dark now and lights blazed from the technocrats' houses, but the sense of enchantment was lost.

At home she flung off her coat and went to the kitchen to fetch a drink. Grumps was at the table making scones. He had attached a thick metal hook to his arm and plunged it into a bowl of flour and margarine. His arm vibrated slightly as the hook worked the dough. "Good evening, Miss Fleur," he said. She ignored him and went to the fridge, slamming the door behind her. By the time Grumps had raised his features into an expression of surprise, she had left the room.

Her mother stopped her as she was halfway up the stairs. "Are you all right?"

Fleur nodded, tight-lipped, and carried on up without looking at her mum. Mrs. Bell made to follow her, then thought better of it. Whatever had happened, it would no doubt soon blow over.

Fleur lay on her bed and seethed. Yet again Marcia had been horrible to her. Why did she put up with it? So that she could boast about her friend the technobrat and experience the latest technology before anyone else? She was ashamed to admit this was true. On the other hand . . . Fleur mentally ticked off Marcia's good qualities. She made Fleur laugh (sometimes even when the joke was at Grumps' expense); though she was sharp-tempered, it never lasted long; she was full of energy; she made wonderful things; she was pretty; and she took Fleur on simulated adventures. The underwater trip had been fun. . . .

But that isn't enough to be her friend anymore, Fleur told herself angrily. She wondered whom she could call to tell how unpleasant Marcia had been. It was hard to think of anyone. She had been so flattered by Marcia's attentions that she had neglected her other friends. They would probably laugh at her comeuppance now.

"House," she said. A green light appeared on the wall beside the door. "Is Gavin back?"

"No," said the house, "I believe he is out with your father."

"I know that!" she snapped. "Switch off."

There was a knock at the door. It had to be her mum. Mrs. Bell came in, a concerned look on her face, and sat at the end of the bed. "Shall I rub your feet?" she said, and gently kneaded the soles of her daughter's feet until Fleur began to feel like a small child again.

"Mum, why can't we go anywhere?"

Mrs. Bell's hands were still for a moment. She stared at Fleur. "What do you mean? We have holidays, we visit our friends. . . ."

"Not very often! We don't even go to the city, and that's

next door. And Gavin and I never go out on our own. Sometimes I feel cooped up like a stupid animal."

"That's not true, Fleur. You went on your own to Marcia's house today."

"Marcia's house! That's hardly seeing the world!"

Her mum said brightly, "You can go anywhere you want on the gobey—the pyramids, the Taj Mahal . . ."

"But it's not real, is it? And it's always the gobey that decides what it's going to be like. You don't see the ugly bits, or smell anything horrid. . . ."

"You can always ask the gobey to show you."

"It's still not the same!" said Fleur. "And we don't even go anywhere in real life. It's been ages since we went to Scotland to see Gran and Granddad."

Mrs. Bell smiled resignedly. "We have to wait our turn for tickets. You know there's not much fuel."

"There is for Marcia and the rest of the technocrats. It's not fair!" Fleur caught her breath as she realized what she had said.

Her mother stopped massaging altogether and looked at her gravely. "How do you know?" she asked.

Fleur lowered her eyes. She didn't want to relate what had happened at Marcia's house. Mrs. Bell's expression became wistful. Then it changed to the look she used to have when telling Fleur a bedtime story. She gave a sigh.

"When I was your age, Fleur, everything seemed to be collapsing about us. Our food no longer nourished us, we couldn't move for traffic, the rivers and seas were polluted, trees were dying, there were floods and earthquakes and hurricanes and drought. . . . Much of it was our fault. And while people all over the world were getting richer, a lot of the poor were getting poorer. Some people went on buying and buying things they didn't really need as if that were the answer to all our problems.

"My mum and dad did their best. They decided that what really mattered in life was their family, their friends, and helping others. Lots of people thought the same and they tried to live more simply. . . ." She broke off. Fleur's eyes were fixed on her face, which was both thoughtful and sad.

"When I grew up, I didn't think they'd done enough. Your dad thought the same. There were thousands of us, young people . . . we demanded healthy food, clean air, but most of all, a fairer system. There was no gobey, but we had something similar and suddenly the whole world could talk to each other. We didn't want anyone to suffer to produce food or goods for us, whether they lived next door or the other side of the planet. It felt as if everyone was our neighbor.

"Then the petrol began to run out and the real changes began. The air grew cleaner, but we couldn't use our cars anymore or travel long distances. We began to live as we do now, growing our food locally, and working nearby, with people like ourselves."

"But there are still poor people and rich people. Look at the people in the city! And the technocrats have everything." Fleur thought with bitterness of her visit to Marcia.

Her mother stroked her hair. "Did you really think we could have created a perfect world?" She placed her hands in her lap and looked toward the window. "One thing didn't change. We still turned to the government and the scientists to solve most of our problems. It was easier to do that than change ourselves. Many people thought the new technology would be the answer. The robots came and life did become easier . . . in some ways."

"Is that why the technocrats are so important?"

Her mum nodded. "They hold the secrets. They make the technology, they understand it. We let them make the decisions for us so we accept that they have certain privileges, like travel."

"So everyone knows?"

"They don't teach it at the learning center, but you would have found out sooner or later."

There was a moment's silence.

"Marcia thinks we're old-fashioned."

Mrs. Bell gave a wry smile. "We certainly don't live quite as they do." She stood up. "I'm sorry, Fleur," she said softly. "We did our best." She paused at the window, looking out at the night sky as if answers lay beyond the stars. "Gavin and your dad aren't back yet. Do you want something to eat now?"

"I'll wait. But I'm not hungry."

Mrs. Bell bent down and kissed her daughter on the forehead. Her mum seemed so forlorn that impulsively Fleur threw her arms about her neck and kissed her in return. When she was alone again, she hugged her knees to her chest and tried to imagine herself back in the depths of the ocean. Only, this time it would be for real.

CHAPTER 8

There was a disturbance in the house. Glad of a distraction, Fleur ran into the kitchen, where the noise was coming from. Her mum and dad and Gavin were there, their mouths open.

Grumps stood by the table, the dough hook still on the end of his arm, plastered with dollops of flour that were gravitating toward the floor. He didn't notice. His eyes were fixed on a strange white object, about Fleur's height, in the center of the kitchen.

"What a beginning!" exclaimed Mrs. Bell. "I hope it isn't damaged."

The object began to shake itself, throwing off small clouds of white dust.

"I am mortified," said Grumps. "I intended to switch off my mixing mechanism. Instead I seem to have turned it to full speed. I cannot explain why."

Mrs. Bell exchanged a glance with her husband. "You were

taken by surprise, Grumps. It isn't every day we have a new robot in the house. I certainly wasn't expecting one tonight."

The white object continued to shake. A pair of rubbery hands revealed themselves and clapped together tentatively. Large drifts of flour fell to the ground. The hands clapped again.

"Try jumping up and down," said Gavin. The object obeyed and the air was thick with flour. Fleur was appalled at the figure that emerged. She looked at her mum to see her reaction, but Mrs. Bell seemed determined to be positive.

"Wonderful, now we can see you properly. . . . He's very rubbery, isn't he?" she added involuntarily. This was true. The robot's arms and legs, which appeared to be a series of rubber rings, on closer inspection turned out to be single pieces of rubber compressed into a concertina. His body was metal, the color of tarnished bronze. His head was round and rubbery and his neck another series of rubber rings.

"Is this it?" cried Fleur. Her mum looked reprovingly at her. Mr. Bell stepped forward. "Grumps, get a brush and give EGR3 a proper clean. Provided that won't harm your mechanism?" he inquired of the new robot.

"Oh, no, I am very robust."

"It's late," continued Mr. Bell, "and we haven't had supper yet. Let's leave you with Grumps for tonight and we can meet again in the morning."

The butler reappeared with a fine bristle brush and began to sweep away the rest of the flour.

"EGR3 has come to help you, Grumps," said Mrs. Bell. "We want you to teach him everything you know."

"Very well, Mrs. Bell," said Grumps, brushing inside the folds of the new robot's arms with great concentration. "But what I know is rather old-fashioned. I am not like these new 'personal assistant' robots. I don't know about offering advice on your clothes or listening to your problems. . . ."

"We're not expecting you to teach any of that," said Mrs. Bell, trying to keep a straight face.

"Let's eat," said her husband. "Grumps, look after EGR3 tonight. You can clear away the supper dishes tomorrow."

He ushered the others toward the door. "Come on, it's rude to stare," he said to his wife and daughter. Fleur looked at her dad as if he had gone mad. It was only a robot, after all.

"Excuse me," said a quiet voice. "I feel we haven't been properly introduced."

The Bells stopped in their tracks. All four of them stared at EGR3.

"Robot etiquette, lesson one," muttered Gavin. He stepped forward. "Let me introduce you to my mum, she's called Chloe, or rather, Mrs. Bell, and this is my sister, Fleur. My other sister, Charlotte, has gone to bed . . . she's a baby. Everyone—this is EGR3. Professor Ogden says he's the first of a new breed of robots."

"We're delighted to have you here," said Mrs. Bell, smiling. EGR3 extended a hand and she shook it with a sense of bewilderment. Though she always insisted on speaking kindly to robots, it was another thing altogether to be shaking hands with one.

Fleur was looking sullenly at the new arrival. When EGR3 offered her his hand she held back. But as she met his eye, something in the robot's eager gaze prompted her to stretch out her arm. The hand that wrapped itself around hers was surprisingly strong and pliable.

"Hello, Fleur."

"Till tomorrow, then," said Mr. Bell jocularly. He and the children went off to the dining room. Mrs. Bell carried some of the dirty bowls over to the dishwasher.

"Oh, dear," she sighed. "I do hope they get on. It would be such a shame, wouldn't it, if they fought?" Shocked, she realized she was addressing her remarks to the kettle, and hurried out of the kitchen. "*You're* supposed to be the intelligent life around here!" she reminded herself.

* * * * *

Mr. Bell and Gavin took it in turns to recount what had happened at Professor Ogden's house. Fleur only half listened. In her mind she was going over and over her words to Marcia: "I don't expect we'll have an ordinary robot." They certainly didn't. Of course, she was never going to speak to Marcia again, after the way she had behaved. But how could she face her, how could she face anyone, with a round-headed rubber midget in attendance?

73

"I said, what do you think, Fleur?" repeated her father.

"Hmm?"

"What should we call him? The new robot."

It was on the tip of her tongue to say she couldn't care less. Then an image came to her of the look in EGR3's eyes as he held her hand. "Eager," she heard herself saying.

"Eager?"

"That's just what he's like," said Gavin excitedly. "Eager to meet you, eager to help, eager to learn . . ."

"You should have seen him on the hoverbus," mused Mr. Bell. "He would have shaken hands with everyone if we hadn't stopped him."

"Eager it is, then," said Mrs. Bell. "We'll have to ask him if he likes it." For once her family did not chorus: "But he's just a machine!"

"I'll go and ask him now," said Gavin, who found himself feeling protective of the new robot. He was, after all, partly responsible for bringing EGR3 to the house.

Grumps was introducing EGR3 to the kitchen appliances. "This is the refrigerator. It looks after the food that needs to be kept cool. It doesn't say anything," he said in a confidential tone, "but it writes messages to let us know when food is running out." They moved to the oven. "Very clever," said the butler, still in a low voice. "Cooks the food exactly as you want it. It creates menus too." Gavin came into the room.

"And this," Grumps added, raising his voice dramatically, "is the kettle." He seemed to be waiting for something.

"He wants you to say hello," prompted Gavin.

"How do you do?" said EGR3. The kettle made no response.

Grumps looked pleased and showed EGR3 a small room off the kitchen. "Washing and drying machines. They'll explain everything you need to know," he said airily.

Back in the kitchen he pointed to a large cupboard. "Pantry. For the food that doesn't go in the refrigerator."

"We need carrots," said the cupboard in a high fluting voice.

"The pantry and the refrigerator are connected to the local food store. They can order food directly when we run out. But Mr. and Mrs. Bell like to check the orders before they go."

"I should think so!" said Gavin. "Once they ordered twelve dozen eggs between them."

The robots, realizing he was still there, looked expectantly at him. "I've come to tell you we've a new name for you, EGR3. If you like it, of course. We thought we'd call you Eager."

EGR3's rubbery features were expressionless.

"Eager: ardent, keen and enthusiastic," said Grumps, who had an inbuilt dictionary.

"Really?" said EGR3. "Does it really mean all those things?"
Gavin nodded.

"I like it," said EGR3.

"Euphoric," said Gavin.

"Would you like a cup of tea?" said a voice. "I am plumbed into the water supply and can fill myself automatically."

Grumps hurried off to the sink. "Don't worry," whispered

Gavin in response to EGR3's startled look. "I'll explain later. "Night, Eager."

It was very quiet in the big kitchen after the boy left. Eager looked around the walls at the shiny appliances, which seemed to stare blankly back at him. He heard a low rumble and turned to see Grumps approaching.

"Time to recharge my batteries," said the butler. "Excuse me if I don't show you the rest of the house. I'm sure the family will not mind if you explore it on your own." He turned toward the far corner of the room, then paused, swiveling his head round to face Eager again.

"It is nighttime, I trust?"

Eager was taken aback. Of course it was nighttime. It was dark outside and Grumps had just prepared supper. The rubbery rings of his neck tilted to one side to send extra thinking power to his brain. Mr. Bell had explained on the hoverbus that Grumps sometimes became confused. Perhaps this was what he had meant.

"It is nighttime," he said, copying the firm tones that Professor Ogden used for making important statements.

Grumps held his eye for a second longer as if he was suspicious. "You are a robot," he said at last, "so you cannot lie. Therefore I must believe you. Excuse me."

Eager reflected. Other robots, he knew, were programmed to tell the truth. But he had been designed to learn for himself and make his own decisions. If he wanted to tell a lie he could. He had no wish to lie. Yet the thought struck him that by not telling Grumps the truth—that he could lie if he wished—he *had* lied, in a sort of way. He raised his eyes to the window and the darkness beyond. Living in the real world was far more complicated than he had imagined.

Meanwhile Grumps had disappeared. Eager searched him out at the opposite end of the kitchen. As soon as he saw him he cried, "Are you all right?" There was no reply. The butler stood in a corner, as blank-faced and inanimate as the kitchen appliances. A thin cable dangled from his side and fed at the other end into the wall. Eager realized that Grumps must have turned himself off while he was recharging; nonetheless he felt uncomfortable at the sight and moved away.

To all intents and purposes, Eager was alone in the kitchen. He hurried over to the door, which opened soundlessly at his approach, and peered down the hallway. It was empty and silent. The family must have gone to bed. He had no wish to venture any further, as Grumps had suggested. After his small room at the top of Professor Ogden's house, this new home seemed huge and unwelcoming.

Eager went back into the kitchen and found a spot from which the butler was out of view. He would turn down his power, just enough to keep his thoughts ticking over, and use the dark hours to reflect on all that had happened to him. He wondered what Professor Ogden was doing, now that he no longer had to visit the small room above his laboratory in the middle of the night. An image of the professor's slow smile drifted before him, and Eager quickly turned his mind to other things.

CHAPTER 9

The next day began well with a familiar breakfast of cereal and toast. There were even hard-boiled eggs. Eager, who was clearly taking his new name very seriously, hovered enthusiastically around the table while Grumps kept up a running commentary: "Master Gavin likes his egg softly done—he would prefer the one on the right. Pour the coffee from a height and you won't spill it. . . ."

Mr. Bell had soon had enough and was about to tell them to be quiet when his wife pressed his arm. "At least they're getting on. This stage won't last, I'm sure," she whispered. He looked at her in despair. Just when he had thought the whole family was beginning to behave rationally, they ended up pussyfooting around two robots instead of one.

After breakfast the children and their parents went upstairs to work and Grumps was left to care for Charlotte. This was the first time Eager had met a baby. He had been expecting a smaller version of Gavin or Fleur but this child was round and dimpled, and when Grumps sat her on the floor she looked as if she might tip over backward at any minute.

Charlotte lifted her eyes to Eager: unlike other humans, she showed no curiosity or suspicion in her gaze. He noticed that she looked at everything in the same uncritical way, except when Grumps played a game of hide-the-teddy-behind-my-back. Her eyes flew open in surprise and delight every time he made the teddy reappear.

Eager's head tilted to one side as he watched this puzzling behavior. Once, Professor Ogden had asked him what would happen to the furniture in the house if Eager went out for a walk.

"Why, nothing," said Eager, who thought it was a very silly question. "It would still be there when I came back. Unless someone had stolen it, for example, but then I wouldn't know until I returned home."

The professor, he remembered, had leant back and exchanged delighted looks with his research assistants. Eager had concluded that this understanding was somehow extremely important if you were to live in the real world. Yet here was a human baby who seemed not to know that if you hid a toy behind your back it would still be there a second later.

What astonished him even more was the number of times Grumps was prepared to play the game. At last he cried in exasperation, "Aren't you bored?"

Grumps looked up at Eager, the teddy dangling from his

chunky fingers. "Bored?" he repeated, as if he had never heard the word before. "I am not designed to be bored. I am built to have infinite capacity for any task required of me."

"Well, I'm not!" retorted Eager. "I'm bored just watching you. I'm designed that way so that I'll always want to be learning something new."

Grumps straightened up. "Like humans," he said. Charlotte, having lost sight of the teddy altogether, turned to another toy.

"My patience makes me a good teacher," continued the butler.

Eager hung his head while he thought a little. "If you'll pardon my saying so, Grumps, I should give up. That baby will never understand."

At the end of the morning, to Eager's relief, Mrs. Bell took Charlotte away while Grumps demonstrated how to prepare a salad for lunch. He watched as Eager chopped tomatoes.

"I sprinkle a little of this on them," he said, holding up a thin container marked SALT. "Never to be confused with that—he pointed to a larger pot marked SUGAR. "The humans get very upset if you do."

"I'm not surprised," said Eager. "Sweet and salty are very different." He noticed that Grumps looked blank. "I have elementary taste buds, so I can tell."

"I haven't," said Grumps. "Of course, I'm old-fashioned. I simply copy what Mrs. Bell does. No one complains . . . at least, not often."

"Your cooking smells good. I have a basic sense of smell too, you see . . . it helps me understand the human world."

Surprisingly, Grumps nodded. "I can smell three things. One of them is smoke."

Before Eager could ask what the other two were, a lilting female voice said, "So, we have a new worker. I'm glad I don't have a body if this is what robots are looking like these days."

Eager was hunting around for the speaker. "It's the house," said Grumps. "I rarely reply. There is little to say, I always find." He began to pour oil for the mayonnaise into the mixer.

"How do you do?" said Eager, in the direction of the green light beside the door.

"*Hell*-o. If you have any questions, I'm the person to ask."

"Person!" muttered Grumps, turning on the mixer to full speed. It was some seconds before there was quiet again.

"Thank you," said Eager, "I'll remember that."

The green light flickered and went out. Eager balanced another tomato on the chopping board. "If you don't mind, Grumps," he said, "I'd like to keep you as my teacher."

The butler was spooning golden dollops into a jug. "As you wish."

■ ■ ■ ■ ■

The house turned itself on in the hallway as Fleur and Mrs. Bell came downstairs, closely followed by Mr. Bell and Gavin.

"Please, Mum, it's not fair," Fleur was saying.

"I've just seen the new robot," said the house.

"We are having a dispute, don't interrupt," said Gavin.

"I thought you should know," persisted the house, "that I wouldn't trust my children with that thing. He looks as if he couldn't defend himself from a paper bag."

"Exactly!" cried Fleur, leading the way into the dining room. "So he can't possibly take us to the learning center. Ever!"

The rest of the family sat down at the table. "I agree with you, Fleur, Eager is probably not the ideal bodyguard, but he should still go with you this once," said Mrs. Bell firmly. "He might have to take you or collect you one day in an emergency."

Fleur groaned. "It might only be once . . . but I'll never live it down."

Mrs. Bell shot a look at her husband that said, "I'd thought we'd solved the robot problem."

"Fleur," said her dad, "Eager is here to help Grumps, and us, remember. Though it strikes me he's a different kettle of fish, too clever for most of the jobs we have for him. Some of his responses are positively humanlike. Do you know, he brought me up a coffee this morning and before I knew it we were chatting about my work. I ended up recommending a book on architecture. To a robot!"

"He certainly has an inquiring mind," agreed Mrs. Bell, who preferred a cup of Darjeeling midmorning and had struggled to answer Eager's questions about tea production.

"But he *isn't* human, Dad. He's weird, even for a robot." Fleur threw herself into her chair. "I can't go out with him, I'll look such a clone. Why can't you or Mum be a technocrat so we can buy a proper robot like Boadicea?"

"It's too late for that," said her mother briskly. "If we'd wanted to become scientists we would have done so by now." She looked at the clock on the wall. "Looks like you'll need to leave straight after lunch."

Fleur was at her sulkiest when she, Gavin and the two robots set off for the learning center. "It's worse than this morning," she grumbled, as Grumps introduced his protégé to the neighborhood.

"This is the professional quarter," he was saying. "We live here because the Bells are professional people. Every town has one, I understand. Mrs. Bell's parents live in a professional quarter in Scotland."

Grumps pointed out the factories and offices, but Eager was interested in everything—the trees, the grass that poked up from the pavement, the rusty iron railing outside an office block, an old signpost saying MOTORWAY.

"It's all real," he kept saying. Grumps had never given any thought to such a matter but he stopped until Eager was ready to move on. The children waited resignedly.

"I can't believe it," sighed Fleur. "Even Charlotte walks quicker than this."

At last they reached the learning center. "You can leave us now," said Fleur to Grumps, as she did most days.

"I would not be doing my duty if I did not come to the steps with you," replied Grumps, as he always did.

"We'll leave Eager on guard at the gate, then." She flashed a dazzling smile that reminded Gavin of Marcia. "Very clever," he told his sister as they walked toward the entrance.

Eager watched them go. He was fascinated by the people passing, of all shapes and sizes and ages and colors. As his brain began to distinguish one human from another, he realized that there were robots too. Some reminded him of Grumps; others were faster and more flexible. One in particular was tall and very beautiful, it seemed to him, with curvy limbs and golden metal. He felt an impulse to run up to her and make friends but she walked straight by, as if she had not seen him. Perhaps she didn't recognize him as a robot.

He knew, because Professor Ogden had said so, that until humans made robots with artificial skin and muscles he was more lifelike than any other machine. It was true that he could bend and twist and stretch, and screw his face into hundreds of expressions, but he didn't look like a human or a regular robot. He noticed that people were beginning to stare at him and shrank back against the outside wall.

Grumps reappeared and led him beyond the learning center in the direction of the technocrats' quarter. They stopped outside the high wall that surrounded the area. "Fleur's friend Marcia lives here," volunteered the butler. Eager peered through the gateway at the rows of houses. "Why is there a wall?" he asked. "Are they in prison?"

"I don't think so," said Grumps.

They were about to return home when a van with an open back drove out of the gate. Two robots sat side by side in the front. As the vehicle passed them, Eager and Grumps noticed a third robot lying motionless in the back. The engine spluttered and stalled. The robots at the front must have restarted it because a moment later the van drove off, belching gray smoke from the exhaust.

"What happened?" asked Eager.

"The petrol is very low-quality. It comes from an impure source."

"I meant the robot," said Eager. "Why was it lying down?"

Grumps started to walk in the direction of home. "They had cut off its power supply," he said matter-of-factly.

"Who?"

"Its owners."

"Why?"

"In all likelihood they no longer had need of its services," said Grumps.

"No longer had need . . . but what exactly did they do?" said Eager.

"I understand that newer robots are designed to require very little energy. They are powered by radio waves, whereas I rely on batteries, which I recharge every night. Should you remove my batteries I would no longer function. In the same way, if one stops transmitting power to these other robots, they are incapable."

"Dead," whispered Eager.

"I beg your pardon?"

"Dead, like humans when they reach the end of their life."

Grumps had nothing to say to this. It was outside the realms of his experience. Instead he remarked, as if discussing the weather, "I believe Mr. and Mrs. Bell were going to do the same to me, remove my batteries, that is."

Eager felt overcome by a sense of confusion. He hardly dared move. He too was powered by radio waves. Did this mean the Bells would one day cut off his energy supply? He wondered whether Professor Ogden would be an accomplice to the act.

"Doesn't it give you a funny feeling, to see another robot . . . like that?"

"Why should I feel anything?" asked the butler. "Obviously, I have not been programmed to respond to this situation. I have no feelings about it at all, funny or otherwise."

They walked the rest of the way home in silence. Eager was no longer fascinated by the objects and materials on his route. Before, they had seemed to call out to him to look, to smell, to marvel. Now they appeared squalid and lifeless, as if the color had drained out of them. The world suddenly was remote and unfriendly, and he felt as if he did not care what happened next. There was nothing more to explore, nothing more to experience.

* * * * *

"Has anything happened?" Mrs. Bell asked Grumps as Eager sloped off toward the kitchen. "He doesn't have his usual bounce." The butler did not know how to reply. "I am showing him all I know," he said simply.

Eager stood in the center of the room and surveyed the domestic appliances. He wondered what they felt about coming to the end of their life. "Excuse me," he said politely to the fridge. "Do you know anything about death?" Too late, he remembered that the fridge did not speak. A message scrolled across the fridge's door. "We seem to have run out of death. Shall I order some?"

"No," Eager said abjectly. He walked along the hallway to the bottom of the stairs. He had not yet been to the top of the house, and perhaps he would find Mr. or Mrs. Bell there. But all the rooms on the upper floors were empty.

Eager was about to go back down when he noticed a small flight of steps. He climbed them and found himself outside a door. It sensed his arrival and slid open. Inside the room were a large screen and a couple of chairs. "The gobetween," said the robot to himself. The screen flickered into action.

An odd-looking potbellied man was sitting under a gnarled tree. Eager was astonished to see that the man was wrapped in a white sheet. He had hoisted it about his thighs in order to sit comfortably on the grass. Behind him rose a cluster of stone buildings, each with many steps and columns. They reminded Eager of the learning center.

"You will need glasses to join me," said the man. Eager

understood that he was talking about a simulation. "I don't need them," he said. "I can switch myself into simulation mode." The next moment he was stepping into the scene. It was a hot day and the colonnaded buildings looked almost white in the sunlight. He sat down on the grass, which was turning brown in places.

"Good afternoon," he greeted the man.

"Is it?" asked the other.

"I . . . I don't know," stammered Eager.

"Well, is it good, or isn't it?"

"No, it is not good. It was earlier on, but now I'm feeling very confused. I don't know about death."

"What is there to know?"

Eager was finding all these questions rather trying. "I was hoping you would tell me."

"How can we know about death before we die? Don't you want to know about life?"

"I hadn't really thought about it."

"Well," said the man, "how can you have a good death without a good life?"

Eager pondered. The man in the sheet seemed very keen that things should be "good." He decided to ask him what he meant by that.

"At last," said the man, permitting himself a smile. But instead of telling Eager he asked, "What do *you* mean by good?"

"Professor Ogden," Eager said without hesitating. "He

made me," he explained. "He is good. He's never harmed me and he's very kind."

The man stroked his jaw. "Hmm?"

"And the Bells are very good. They're concerned about me and I try to do my best for them. So that is one way to be good, I suppose."

"Is it important to be good?" asked the philosopher.

Eager stared at him. "I want to be like Professor Ogden," he said hotly. "I don't think I should like to be bad at all. People will be unhappy, and if people are unhappy then the world will be an unhappy place. Like it seemed this afternoon," he added dully.

"Is it important to be happy?"

Eager gave what he hoped was a frosty look. "I don't think you should go round asking questions like this," he said. "You might give people wrong ideas."

"Without questions, how will we ever know?"

Eager looked suspiciously at the philosopher. "I believe the Bells think I ask too many questions already. Anyway, what's the point of my asking questions if you refuse to answer me?"

A shadow passed across the man's face and he seemed to have difficulty catching his breath. "I'm feeling rather tired," he said. "Perhaps you could come back another day." And before Eager could respond he had faded away.

CHAPTER 18

The days went by and life in the Bell household continued to improve. Meals were on time and the food was no longer surprising. (Though more than one member of the family missed the possibility of having lemon meringue pie for breakfast.)

As for Eager, he had decided that he enjoyed living with the Bells. He liked the way the boy greeted him each day with a chirpy "Morning, Eager," and always offered to explain anything new. Mr. and Mrs. Bell were thoughtful too, although they were both busy. Mrs. Bell in particular often said, with a kind smile that reminded Eager of Professor Ogden, "You will tell us if you're not happy about something, won't you?"

Fleur he found difficult to understand. She wasn't friendly or helpful like Gavin, though nor was she rude. Yet she had a way of looking at him as if she didn't see him that confused and discomfited Eager.

Eager would have liked to return to the learning center where he might meet new people and perhaps talk to the other robots, but after that first visit he was not asked to go again. He helped Grumps about the house, went on errands in the neighborhood, and learnt more about the wider world from visits to the gobetween while the family slept. He began to feel ready for a new challenge.

One morning the children and Grumps went off to the learning center, with Fleur urging the others to hurry to avoid bumping into Marcia.

Mr. Bell had a meeting at the site of the new factory and just had time to gulp down a cup of coffee before kissing his wife goodbye. Eager started to clear away the breakfast things.

"Eager," said Mrs. Bell, "I must finish a report today. I'd like you to watch Charlotte for an hour until Grumps gets back." She spoke casually but both she and Eager knew that this was an important step.

"Are you sure?" Eager asked in spite of himself.

"You've been helping Grumps, haven't you? He seems to think you're very good with her. The important thing is to keep an eye on her at all times. Don't let her touch anything sharp or put small objects in her mouth or—"

"Don't worry," interrupted Eager with feeling. "I know all about dangers—cutting things, chemicals, falling . . . I learnt about them during my own infancy at the professor's house."

"Good," said Mrs. Bell. "Now, if she cries—you know the grizzly sort of cry she makes . . ."

"She's probably thirsty, hungry or tired, or has a dirty nappy."

Mrs. Bell smiled. "I see you've learnt a lot already. I'll leave you to it. She's had a good breakfast but if she does seem hungry later you can give her a biscuit. You'll find the biscuits in a tin in the pantry."

She handed him Charlotte, who gurgled happily and tried to pull his nose. "You're obviously a natural," laughed Mrs. Bell. Nonetheless, a qualm seized her at the last moment. Grumps had helped to bring up Fleur and Gavin and she didn't think twice about leaving him with Charlotte, but Eager was still an unknown quantity.

"Eager," she said firmly, "if you're in any doubt at all, if there's any problem, you must call me at once."

"Yes, Mrs. Bell."

Charlotte was so absorbed in the nose-pulling game that she didn't notice her mother leaving. After eight pulls Eager held her at arm's length. "Time for something else. I'm not Grumps," he told her, and carried her into the living room to find some toys. He took out some wooden bricks and built elaborate towers with balustrades. To his immense frustration she knocked them over each time.

Charlotte, he discovered, loved to make a noise and for a long time she banged an irregular rhythm on a battered tin drum. Then, without warning, she dropped the drumstick and her face puckered.

"Nahhhh! Nahhh!" It was the grizzle Mrs. Bell had reminded him about. He carried the baby into the kitchen and offered her a bottle. She pushed it away with unexpected strength. "Nahhhh! Nahhhhh!" It was too soon to change her nappy and she didn't seem to be tired. "Biscuit?" suggested Eager. The grizzling stopped. Eager sat Charlotte down on the floor and went to the pantry. There was a large round tin just inside the door. He opened it and took out a biscuit that was golden on one side and bright red on the other. He offered it to Charlotte.

"Mmm." She reached for the biscuit. He handed it to her with the prettier red side uppermost, but instead of eating the biscuit she waved it in the air and held it out to Eager. He began to wonder about human intelligence.

"Don't offer it to me," he said, "I just gave it to you."

Charlotte put the biscuit to her mouth and sank her small ivory teeth into it. She chuckled and waved the biscuit at him once more.

Eager closed the lid and returned the tin to the pantry. The door closed behind him as he stopped dead in his tracks. When he had left Charlotte with the biscuit she had been wearing a white top and pale yellow trousers. Now both were decorated in a livid red pattern. The same red was in evidence across her face, and as he moved closer he saw that it was in her hair as well. There was also a piece of biscuit suspended on the side of her head. This confused him since the law of gravity suggested that the biscuit should have fallen to the ground by now. He took it between his fingers and felt a slight resistance as he pulled it away from her hair. The downside, the red part, was sticky.

Charlotte had evidently taken a large bite of the biscuit and was munching contentedly. The rest of it was squashed in her tiny fists and something red and syrupy oozed between her fingers. This biscuit did not fit Eager's understanding of biscuit. Biscuits were hard. They made crumbs. They were not soft and they did not exude sticky lumps.

He stared at Charlotte in dismay. He had never seen her in such a mess! Grumps could be back at any moment and, worse, Mrs. Bell might come downstairs to check on his progress. The thought of failure was intolerable to him. He would never be trusted with the baby again. It surprised him to realize how much he had enjoyed the morning. He would have to remove the red stuff before anyone saw her. But how?

He knew that Charlotte had a bath every night but this was midmorning. Besides, she was covered in the sticky stuff—clothes, hair, face, the whole of her needed washing. He remembered his first evening in the house, when Grumps had shown him the washing and drying machines. "They'll tell you what to do," Grumps had said. Scooping up Charlotte and holding her at arm's length, he carried her to the laundry room. He noticed yet more hair stuck together in red clumps. There was even a blob of red on the end of her eyelashes.

The washing machine was activated by his approach. "What do you wish to wash?" it asked in an officious voice.

"A baby."

The machine considered for a moment. "I have never

washed a baby before," it admitted, "so I am unable to advise you. Is it heavily soiled, lightly soiled or worn once?"

"Heavily soiled," said Eager decisively.

"Natural fabric or synthetic?"

"Natural." Eager was feeling pleased with himself. This was obviously the right thing to do.

"Delicate or—"

"Delicate," said Eager. There was no doubt that babies needed to be handled carefully.

"Then I recommend a long gentle wash with a mild detergent followed by a short spin."

Eager knew that chemicals could harm children. "I believe detergent is bad for babies."

"Very well. I shall use soap flakes. Place the item in the drum."

"Are you sure?" asked Eager. The door seemed rather small.

"Of course I am," replied the washing machine, somewhat irritably, Eager thought.

The door clicked open and Eager lowered Charlotte into the drum of the machine. She seemed to be enjoying the game and kicked her legs in pleasure.

"*What are you doing?*" thundered a voice. Eager looked over his shoulder. It was Grumps. The older robot appeared to be under so much strain that Eager was afraid he might explode.

"*Remove that baby at once!*"

Eager experienced a confused sensation like the one he had felt when he saw the dead robot in the van. He lifted Charlotte out of the drum and handed her into Grumps' outstretched arms.

"Don't you know . . . the first . . . law . . . of . . . robot . . . behavior?"

Before Eager could reply, Grumps unleashed a torrent of words. "Never . . . ever . . . in all my career . . . to harm a baby . . . We are programmed to care for humans . . . It is contrary to our behavior . . ."

Eager wished he could block out the sound of Grumps' voice. In fact, he could have put up a barrier between his ears and the sound but something told him this would be wrong. He stood there as the words washed over him until eventually he managed to say, "I am not programmed like you."

Grumps stopped in midsentence.

"I mean," continued Eager, "of course I know the laws of robot behavior . . ."

"Well?"

"A robot must never harm, or allow harm to be done to, a human being. A robot must never do anything that might endanger a human being. A robot must not harm itself or another robot, unless the other robot is endangering a human being." He broke off, although there were several other laws to recite. "The thing is, I am not programmed to obey rules. I am programmed to learn and to think for myself. It is my choice how I behave."

He could see that Grumps did not understand him and added miserably, "I thought the washing machine would know what to do."

Grumps said nothing. Charlotte hit him playfully on the cheek and automatically he began to jig her up and down. She squealed with laughter.

"I'm sorry," said Eager. "I don't want to harm her. I've learnt a lesson and I'll never put Charlotte in danger again. Please don't tell anyone."

"I am unable to tell a lie," intoned Grumps. "But if nobody asks me I shall have no reason to speak of this matter."

"Thank you," said Eager. The dazed feeling still overwhelmed him. To think he had nearly harmed Charlotte! He had only a vague idea what might have happened to her in the machine, yet he could tell by Grumps' reaction that it would have been very nasty. One day he would find out; for the time being he couldn't bear to contemplate it. He followed Grumps back into the kitchen.

"It all started to go wrong when I gave her the biscuit," he pleaded. "It was a funny sort of biscuit."

Grumps examined the red blobs on Charlotte's jumper. "Jam tart," he said. "I made some yesterday and left them in the pantry."

"Ah," said Eager, and thought, not for the first time, that real life was very confusing.

■ ■ ■ ■ ■

That night, after the family had gone to bed, Eager went to the top of the house to visit the philosopher. All day he had not been feeling his usual self. He knew that nothing had happened to injure him and that he was functioning normally, but ever since the affair with the washing machine he had a strong sense of something not being right.

The gobetween screen flickered and the grass and the gnarled tree appeared. The philosopher was there, eating a bunch of grapes with much satisfied slurping. Eager sat down opposite him. It was a fine day and Eager just stopped himself from saying "Good afternoon." The man indicated the bowl of fruit but Eager shook his head.

"Well?" said the philosopher, popping three grapes at once into his mouth.

"I've done a terrible thing, and now I have a terrible feeling that won't go away."

"A crime? A misdemeanor?" prompted the philosopher.

"More of an accident. I nearly harmed the baby. . . . It might have been worse than that," he confessed in a low voice.

"An accident?"

"I didn't know the right thing to do," said Eager.

"Do we not all know the right thing to do, in our hearts?" It sounded more of a statement than a question.

Eager hung his head. "I don't know what you mean by 'right.' I didn't mean to hurt her. I just didn't know that washing machines are bad for babies."

The philosopher pushed the bowl of grapes away from him

and licked his fingers. "You were ignorant of the facts and now you know better? That is a step toward the good life."

"I wondered when we'd get on to that."

The philosopher fixed his eyes on a point in the distance behind Eager. For a moment the robot wondered what the man could see, since in reality he was looking into the room at the top of the Bells' house. Then he remembered that the philosopher was virtual and only appeared to be seeing.

"You have recognized your ignorance, yet you still feel remorse."

"Remorse?" asked Eager.

"You regret your action?"

"Oh, yes!"

The philosopher spread his hands as if to welcome Eager. "This is virtue. And surely virtue is the key to the good life?"

"So I'm a good robot, after all?"

"Who can know your own heart but yourself?" He closed his eyes as if to terminate the meeting.

"Just one more thing," said Eager, who was feeling a lot better. The philosopher opened his eyes.

"When is a biscuit not a biscuit?"

The philosopher frowned. "Is this a rhetorical question? I don't like riddles."

"It's simple." Eager got up to go. "The answer is, when it's a jam tart."

CHAPTER 11

Marcia was the only technobrat at the learning center to have a BDC4 and she quickly became the center of attention. At first Boadicea accompanied her and returned home, as the other robots did. Then she appeared in a class and helped Marcia with her problem solving. Eventually she stayed with her all day. No one was that surprised since Marcia was bound to be tempted to show off Boadicea. Though soon it became clear that they were inseparable.

Fleur secretly hoped that the novelty would pass, and that Marcia would miss their friendship and apologize for her behavior. Until one morning she spotted Marcia and Boadicea walking side by side. The robot was leaning so that her head was close to Marcia's. Both of them were laughing at something. Fleur recognized the pose instantly. Once she and Marcia must have looked like that—sharing a private joke and ignoring everyone else. But Boadicea, she reminded herself angrily, was a robot!

Even Gavin and his friends were intrigued by the pair. At

lunch they found themselves sitting next to Marcia and the BDC4. The girl had just given her order to the robot waiter when Gavin's friend Omar said loudly, raising his voice half an octave: "And a virtual steak and microchips for the robot!"

Everyone burst out laughing. Marcia appeared not to notice, but Gavin could tell by the flash of her eyes that she had heard. She thinks we're jealous, he thought, and she's probably right. Who would not envy a robot that laughed with you and hung on to your every word? All the same, there was something about Boadicea that made him uncomfortable.

When Gavin told Fleur the story, she opened her eyes wide as if to say "Marcia who?" He felt sorry for her. It couldn't be easy to be replaced in someone's affections by a machine.

That afternoon Fleur had a training session in the swimming pool. It was the last place she expected to see Marcia. Fleur was a strong swimmer, and every so often in a fit of enthusiasm she decided to improve her speed and stamina. Marcia claimed not to like water and preferred gymnastics. Yet there she was, in the next lane, alone. She must be having a private lesson, thought Fleur, but she had no time to stop and look.

At the end of the session Fleur hauled herself out of the water and pulled off her goggles just as Marcia touched the end of the pool. It was then that Fleur noticed Boadicea leaning over the edge.

"That arm action was a lot better. But try and relax into the stroke. Two more lengths."

The robot spoke with authority and to Fleur's astonishment Marcia flipped around to swim another length of the pool.

Fleur could hardly stand there in a dripping wet swimming costume. She went into the changing room and took a long time to shower and dress. Her mind was so distracted that she fumbled with her clothes. She came out of the cubicle just as Marcia stepped from the shower, where Boadicea was waiting to wrap her in a microabsorbent robe that hung like silk.

"Hi, Fleur," said Marcia, flicking her long hair over the collar of the robe. "Haven't seen you for ages. I was worried you might be ill, but everyone said you were OK."

Although she didn't show it, Fleur was pleased that Marcia had been concerned and part of her relented. She was about to say something friendly in return when the robot spoke.

"Did you see Marcie swim?" she said in her slow drawl. "Her freestyle has improved no end."

"Thanks," said Marcia.

Fleur gaped. She had never expected to hear Marcia thank a robot. Perhaps Marcia noticed her amazement for she said, "You know, I'm beginning to understand how your family treats Grumps so politely. It's ridiculous, of course, he's stupid, but Boadicea is different. She really understands me, don't you, Bo?"

"I'm your best friend," said the robot.

"She is!" said Marcia. "She's so aware. Go on, ask her something."

Fleur mumbled her reluctance.

"Anything at all," urged Marcia.

"What's the capital of Uruguay?"

"Very funny," laughed Boadicea. "You know that's not at all what Marcie meant. As a matter of fact, I've no idea. But it sounds a lovely place to visit. If you could go anywhere in the world, Fleur, where would you choose?"

"Japan," said Fleur without hesitation.

"Fascinating," said Boadicea. "You should go when there's a festival."

"I'll have to wait a lifetime for the chance to go there," said Fleur with a touch of bitterness.

The robot grimaced. "That's a shame. But people like Marcie's dad will soon perfect new sorts of fuel. You're a wonderful swimmer, you know. I was admiring your technique. . . ."

The conversation became too much for Fleur to bear. "I've got to go. See you around." With disregard for the slipperiness of the floor, she ran to the exit.

* * * * *

After she arrived home Fleur sat brooding in her room. "Robot by name, friend by nature" was how LifeCorp described the BDC4. She had hankered after such a robot ever since she first heard the slogan on the gobetween. Yet Boadicea and her clever ways disturbed her. She had learnt from the family discussions about Grumps that robots were programmed to behave in ways to please humans. Why should she feel alarmed because Boadicea did it so well?

Fleur went upstairs to the top of the house. The gobetween started to throw virtual rose petals into the air as she approached. "Get me Sarupa," she said. It would be late in Bombay but the family never went to bed early.

Sarupa's bedroom filled the screen. In the foreground was a low wooden settee, piled high with brightly patterned cushions. Sarupa was curled up on the settee, her arms outstretched, a bronze-colored BDC4 by her side.

"Hello, Fleur," she said excitedly. "How are you doing? You look a bit glum."

Fleur struggled for words. She had been ready to tell Sarupa all about Boadicea. It was a shock to see her with a BDC4 of her own. Sarupa's dad was a technocrat and very rich, but unlike the Morrises the family didn't rush to buy the latest technology.

"I'm fine," Fleur said. "I didn't know you had a new robot."

"Two weeks. That's why I haven't called. We've been so busy together. Look, what do you think?" Sarupa held out her hands, palms uppermost. Fleur studied the intricate copper tracery. It was impossible to see where it began and ended. "It's beautiful," she said. "Did your sister do it?"

Sarupa threw back her head and laughed. "No! It was Badupca, here. Tell me, isn't this amazing? No one showed her how. She just prepared the henna and did it."

"She must have picked it up from somewhere," said Fleur, thinking of Eager and his ability to learn.

Sarupa shook her head. "She came straight from the factory. Now, have LifeCorp programmed all their robots to do hand painting?" She laughed again, at the absurdity of the idea. The robot made a gesture of impatience.

"I'm sorry, Fleur, Badupca hasn't finished. She likes us to chat while she's working so I had better go. Call me again, OK?"

"OK," said Fleur.

⁜ ⁜ ⁜ ⁜ ⁜

The following morning Grumps cleared away the breakfast table with a heavy air. He answered Eager's questions in monosyllables and sounded more than usually morose. At midday Eager found the butler at the kitchen sink, looking out over the garden and talking to the kettle.

"I've tried everything," he was saying, "her favorite pudding, polishing her shoes, flowers in her room. All to no avail."

"I am plumbed in and can fill myself automatically," trilled the kettle.

"It used to be simple in the old days. When she cried I would find a toy to amuse her or give her a sweet. But nowadays nothing seems to work. Everything's changed. It always does."

Eager did not like to interrupt, but the butler sounded so depressed that he wanted to help. "Is anything the matter?"

Grumps took a moment to swivel his head round. "We were just talking about Miss Fleur," he said. "She's unhappy at the moment and there's nothing I can do about it."

Eager considered this. If Gavin or Mrs. Bell was unhappy he was certain he would notice, but Fleur never chatted to him the way that they did. She often appeared quiet and aloof to him.

"Are you sure?" he said. "I mean, that she's unhappy?"

Grumps nodded. "I've known her since birth," he droned, "I can tell. And if Miss Fleur is unhappy, I am unhappy."

Seeing the butler so miserable gave Eager an uncomfortable sensation. After a moment's reflection he identified it as feeling unhappy because Grumps was unhappy because Fleur was unhappy . . . Eager checked his thoughts. The chain could go on forever until the whole world was unhappy! Though he couldn't resist wondering who would be sad on his behalf. The image of Professor Ogden, then Gavin, came to mind, the two of them looking anxiously at him. It was, in a way, an agreeable thought.

The kettle brought him back to the present moment. "How many cups do you require?"

"I fear there is nothing we can do," said Grumps.

Eager believed in taking action. "I'll talk to her. She might tell me what the matter is; then we'll be able to help."

Grumps turned back to the window. "She's walking down the garden," he said. "Always a bad sign."

Without waiting to find out what the butler meant, Eager

hurried out of the house. He often wandered down to the vegetable patch. Grumps had identified for him the different vegetables growing there and he liked to observe their progress, although there was not a great deal to see at this time of year. He had never gone as far as the wild bit at the furthest end of the garden. Fleur was just ahead of him, wading through some tall grass.

A ball floated over the top of the hedge that divided the garden from its neighbor. Eager was not surprised to see it. He often glimpsed Sphere through the windows of the house or when he was out on an errand. If he was unsure which road to take, the ball sometimes glided ahead of him, along what always turned out to be the right path. Eager felt encouraged by its presence.

"I want to talk to Fleur," he said in a low voice, though he sensed that Sphere already knew this. The ball pulsated with light and drifted into the trees next door.

The robot had almost reached the bottom of the garden when he became aware of a powerful smell, a heavy sweet perfume that reminded him of the incense sticks Mrs. Bell liked to burn in the bathroom. It was coming from a bush with long prickly leaves. Among the leaves were green stems weighted with small yellow flowers. The scent came from these flowers.

He was amazed. The plant seemed to him to be two different specimens—the dark spiky leaves repelling onlookers, and the bright yellow flowers beguiling with their smell. Many things in the real world, from ladles to toothbrushes, struck him as extraordinary at first until he discovered what they were for. But he couldn't work out why this plant should be so dual-natured.

"It's got a long name I can't remember," said Fleur's voice behind him. "I think it's magical. In the winter it looks like holly; then in the spring you get sunshine-yellow flowers." For a moment or two they stood side by side, admiring the bush. Then Eager noticed that Fleur was eyeing him intently.

"You like beautiful things, don't you?" she said. "I don't understand how."

"How what?" he asked politely.

"How a robot can appreciate beauty. I can understand programming a robot so that it doesn't like the look or smell of certain things. You wouldn't want one to go and buy moldy apples, for example."

"Certainly not," said Eager.

"But what you have is something more. You seem to get real pleasure from things. Gavin says it's because you have proper feelings."

Eager had not been expecting to talk about himself. He wondered how he might turn the conversation round to Fleur's unhappiness. Though at the moment she appeared more pensive than sad.

"Do you like swimming?"

"Swimming?" said Eager. He recalled his simulated visits to rivers and seas. "It's not something I think I should try. However, I am a hundred percent waterproof," he added reassuringly.

Fleur scowled. "In my opinion," she said, "robots and water do not mix. The lifesavers at my pool are robotic but they're just minisubmarines with arms."

She swept aside the leaves on a stone bench in the corner and sat down, turning her face to the side. When Eager looked at her again he saw a pattern that was Fleur, yet not Fleur. He began to question the evidence of his eyes. His system worked hard to make sense of the information. Of course! In profile she looked exactly like her mother. He knew that children resembled their parents but he had never seen so faithful a copy before.

"Are you OK?" She was staring at him.

"Yes, thank you. For a moment I thought you weren't who you are, but you are so it's all right."

Her face was transformed again, this time by a frown. "You say the oddest things," she said.

Eager thought it best to change the subject and remembered his mission.

"Grumps thinks you're unhappy," he said.

Fleur snorted. "Trust Grumps. He's not exactly the life and soul of the party himself."

"He's very distressed, I believe."

"If you must know, I'm not unhappy, I'm cross. My best friend prefers her robot to me and I miss having someone to talk to, even if that someone is spoilt and selfish half the time. And my other friends seem to have paired up with each other, and even my gobepals are stepping out with their robots."

This was a lot of information for Eager to take in, but he saw a parallel in his own history. "I lost a friend too," he said thoughtfully, "when I left Professor Ogden to come here. I think I understand a little of what you feel."

Fleur looked sharply at him. He had an unpleasant inkling that she was angry. "You're just a robot," she snapped. "How can you have any idea what I'm feeling? I'm not going to start behaving like Marcia with Boadicea. I've got far more sense!"

She rushed past him, causing him to jump out of the way. He watched her run through the vegetable patch and across the lawn to the house. The unhappy feeling that he had had in the kitchen returned. He wished that he and Fleur could be friends and he didn't understand the reason for her outburst. As he stood there, gloomily, the yellow-flowered bush appeared to glow.

"Sphere?" said Eager.

The ball did not reappear, but Eager's mood began to lift. There were too many good things in life, he decided, to be miserable. He headed slowly toward the house, wondering what to tell Grumps.

CHAPTER 12

It rained heavily in the night, and the morning was cold and overcast. Gavin and Fleur walked in silence to the learning center, followed by Grumps. Gavin was inwardly praying that the weather would clear by the afternoon for his game of liveball. Fleur wondered whether she should have an early lunch and who might go with her.

"Miss Fleur," said Grumps.

"If you're going to tell me I'm daydreaming . . . ," she began tetchily.

"I merely wished to point out that your friend Marcia is approaching."

"She's not my friend," retorted Fleur. Marcia was crossing the courtyard. Boadicea strode alongside, sheltering her from the drizzle with a large silver umbrella. The robot's other hand carried what looked like a box.

The technobrat waved to them as they came through the gates. "Hi, Fleur; hi, Gavin. Do you want to see my pot?"

"Sorry," Fleur said, "but I don't want to miss the start of

interactive maths. See you later, Gavin." She walked on by. Grumps kept his eye on her as she went over to the steps of the main building.

"What about you?" asked Marcia, smiling at Gavin. There was a brightness in her eyes that he hadn't seen before.

He felt awkward. He didn't know Marcia well and he knew even less about art. But she was looking at him so earnestly, almost pleadingly, that it was hard to refuse.

"Er . . . yes." Gavin remembered that she had mentioned the pot before. It must have taken her weeks to make it.

"Boadicea!" said Marcia. "The box."

The robot's eyes were blank as she turned to her mistress. Gavin glanced at Marcia, noting her puzzled frown. With a slow sweep of her arm the BDC4 raised the metal case into the air, her gaze still fixed on Marcia. Gavin knew, sickeningly, that Boadicea was going to swing the case round to hit the girl. He heard Marcia's sharp intake of breath as he lunged forward to grab the robot's arm.

At the same time Marcia clapped her hands together. "Boadicea!" she hissed. The robot froze, then lowered her arm until the metal case was level with her chest.

"She was going to attack you!" said Gavin, his eyes glued to Boadicea in case she made another unexpected move.

"She'd never do that. Would you?" insisted Marcia.

Boadicea smiled. "I'm sorry if I alarmed you. I don't know what came over me, Marcie. I think I'm just so happy about your pot I wasn't concentrating."

Gavin's jaw dropped. He had never before heard a robot talk like this. Nor many humans, luckily. He turned to Marcia to share her reaction, but she was gazing at the robot adoringly. As he looked away Boadicea met his glance; for a split second he saw the unmistakable intelligence in her eyes. And a glimmer of triumph.

"Do you want to see my pot or not?" said Marcia.

Gavin collected himself. Boadicea was expressionless now. He nodded.

Marcia tapped the metal case twice and the lid opened itself. Gavin peered in.

"You can unwrap it."

He pulled back the layers of paper and uncovered a widebellied pot, glazed in white, with a pattern of black zigzags. The inside was a lustrous pink. Gavin wasn't too sure about the pink, but he thought it was a fine pot and told her so.

"Thank you." Her eyes shone brighter than ever and she looked at him with what seemed to be genuine warmth. "I'm taking it home to show my mum and dad. Though they won't be home for ages," she added forlornly.

"Are you sure . . . that is . . ." Gavin was flustered. He wanted to suggest that perhaps it was not safe to go home alone with Boadicea, but he sensed that the robot was watching him intently. It was almost as if she expected him to say that, so instead he said awkwardly, "Well, bye, then."

"Bye, Gavin."

He watched her walk through the gate, Boadicea stepping

gracefully at her side. He and Grumps went to the main building, where he was surprised to find Fleur waiting at the bottom of the steps.

"What was it?" said Fleur.

"Her pot. It's brilliant. Why didn't you stay to look at it?"

Fleur shrugged. "She doesn't need my approval, she has that robot." She saw from Gavin's face that there was more to tell. Her eyes narrowed. "What happened?"

Gavin looked down at his feet. He was not sure now whether he had imagined the whole thing.

"I shall leave you," said Grumps.

"Ask Eager to tell you when it's time to come and meet us," said Gavin. "Bye."

Gavin watched with affection as the elderly robot rolled across the courtyard. Grumps might be old and creaky but he was never violent. The thought made Gavin uneasy.

"Well?" said Fleur.

"Nothing, really. Except Boadicea was sucking up to Marcia. She was so sy . . . syca . . ."

"Sycophantic," said his sister.

Gavin nodded. "It turned my stomach."

"I know what you mean. Got to hurry now. I'll meet you at three-thirty."

He waited until Fleur had disappeared behind the glass doors before jumping down the steps and hurrying to the gates. A plan had formed in his mind. He had kept it from his sister because he knew that she would stop him.

Out in the street he glanced to the left at Grumps' retreating figure. Gavin hoisted his sports bag onto his shoulder and began to run along the pavement in the opposite direction toward the technocrats' quarter. The drizzle had stopped and sunshine poked through the clouds. His sense of purpose turned into excitement and a giddy sense of freedom at being alone in the street.

He wondered what he would do if Boadicea attacked Marcia. The robot was, in effect, a walking suit of armor. Several strong adults would have a job to restrain her. He could go for help, of course, or encourage Marcia to run away. Although she was stubborn enough to insist that nothing was wrong, even if danger was staring her in the face.

He turned a corner. They were ahead of him, strolling toward the compound. Clearly, nothing had happened to Marcia on the way, and the robot appeared to be carrying the metal box with great care. A high wall surrounded the quarter. Gavin was surprised to see that the entrance gates were wide open and that no one was guarding them. Marcia and Boadicea walked through.

Gavin reflected that his job was done. If the BDC4 went berserk there would be neighbors to help Marcia. Yet now that he was there, he felt a great curiosity to enter the compound. Unlike Fleur, he had no technobrat friends and had never visited it before. It would be easy enough to stride through the gates.

As he approached, a yellow sign by the entrance told him of

his mistake. It read in large letters: WARNING, HOT FENCE and had a symbol of fire on it. Gavin groaned in frustration. It made no difference that the gates were open: the entrance itself was protected by an invisible heat barrier. Marcia must have deactivated it somehow, but he would burn himself the moment he came into contact with it.

"Gavin," said a familiar voice.

He started and swung round. "What are *you* doing here?"

Eager looked unusually bashful. "Sphere sent me."

"Sphere? Oh! You mean that floating ball I saw at Professor Ogden's house? What do you mean it sent you? Does it talk?"

Eager frowned as if the questioning was making him uncomfortable. "It doesn't speak like you, but I understand what it wishes me to know. It . . . thinks to me."

"Telepathy," said Gavin. "You know, some people can send their thoughts to others even from the opposite side of the world."

Eager tilted his head. "I'm not sure about that. I know that it happens when we're together."

"What did it say?" said Gavin.

"To come and find you. I knew the way here; Grumps showed me once. That's all," Eager added, seeing Gavin look inquiringly at him.

"Since you're here, can you help me find a way through this hot fence? Perhaps Sphere could tell you," said Gavin jokingly.

Eager walked up to the gates and appeared to be inspecting

the space between them, although there could be nothing to see but air. Gavin kicked his foot impatiently against the side of the pavement, waiting for the robot to come back to him. It was obviously impossible to pass the barrier. You would need a space suit at least to protect you from the heat. Eager's rubber would cook in it.

Just then, Eager stood square-on to the hot fence and stepped forward. "No! Stop!" cried Gavin, but he was too late. The robot entered the compound, where he turned and waved. Gavin ran across the road, his mouth open in disbelief. "Are you all right? How did you do that?"

"There are ways," said Eager, lowering his eyes modestly. "I'll do it again if you wish." He glared resolutely at the hot fence like a warrior before battle and stepped through again.

Gavin could see that there was not so much as a scorch mark on his body. "That's incredible."

"In fact," said Eager, "it's turned off."

Gavin did not know which surprised him more—that the hot fence was not working or that Eager had played a joke on him. He squinted at the entrance and saw that Eager was right. If the barrier had been on he would have seen it shimmering. Was it not working properly? Then why were the gates open? As he followed the robot through he noted that this was the second strange event that morning.

Inside the compound a pathway led uphill. Gavin and Eager began to climb and found themselves wandering between gardens with huge lawns, overlooked by exotic trees. The buildings were like illustrations in a book on the history of architecture. Low ranches enclosed by verandahs, reminding Gavin of hot countries like Australia, were next door to tall houses with narrow windows and chimneys. A house with dark beams and an overhanging top story he recognized as Tudor. Of course, he told himself, none of these houses was old. They had been built at the whim of the technocrats.

"Where are we going?" said Eager.

"I just wanted to look around," said Gavin. "I came here because Marcia's robot was behaving strangely. Perhaps we should find Marcia's house to check she's OK." He stopped walking and scanned the buildings further up the slope. "Fleur told me it's made of glass, so it shouldn't be hard to recognize among this lot. But I don't know where to begin."

Eager's eyesight was as acute as his hearing. He pointed to the right. "Over there, behind those trees."

The glass-sided building actually looked like a modern house. It had a flat roof and stood on slender titanium stilts, giving the impression that the house might sway at any moment. With so much glass it was easy to see in. No one appeared to be home. As they came nearer Gavin could see the furniture on the different floors. It looked ordinary enough—beds, sofas, chairs. On a table downstairs was a metal case.

"This is it," said Gavin. Eager edged closer to the window.

A face appeared and screamed soundlessly. It was Marcia.

118

Gavin pushed in front of the robot and, realizing that she couldn't hear through the glass, waited for her to recognize him. Her mouth sprang shut and she glared. Then her lips began to move, curling and pouting beneath her scowling eyes.

"What . . . are . . . you . . . doing . . . here?" he half-read, half-guessed she was saying.

He shrugged. She looked even more cross and disappeared for a moment. The front door slid open and Marcia stood on the threshold. "What are you doing here? And what on earth is that?" she repeated, glowering at Eager.

Gavin decided that truth was the best policy. "I was worried about you. I thought Boadicea might attack you again so I . . . I followed you home."

"You did *what?*"

"I'd have done it for anyone," he said hastily, worried that she might jump to a wrong conclusion.

"How did you get in?" she asked suspiciously.

"The hot fence was turned off. There was nobody on duty."

Marcia's expression went from scowling to scared. "Don't say they've all gone," she said.

"Who?"

She pursed her lips and didn't answer. "Is that a robot? Or is it Golem?"

Neither Gavin nor Eager knew who Golem was, but from her expression Marcia wasn't being polite. Gavin said brightly, "Let me introduce you to Eager. Eager, this is Marcia."

Eager put out a hand. "How do you do?"

Marcia half recoiled but shook the hand. Boadicea must have done her some good, at least, thought Gavin.

She said in a changed tone, "It was sweet of you to want to protect me, Gavin. Like an old-fashioned knight."

Gavin blushed. He wondered if she was making fun of him.

"Now you're here, do you want some lunch? There's tera-tons of food."

Gavin was hungry and the learning center seemed a long way away. He said thank you and Marcia stepped back to let them into the house.

"Gavin," said Eager without moving, "if you don't mind, I would like to explore a little."

"I suppose it's not much fun watching people eat," said Gavin, glancing at the time on his jinn. "See you at the gate at one-fifteen."

He waved goodbye to the robot and followed Marcia down the hallway. He could not resist peering left and right. They passed a living room that glowed a dark shade of red, the color appearing to pour out from the walls. Marcia noticed his interest and remarked, "It's a bit much for the daytime, isn't it?" as she adjusted a control panel beside the door.

She led the way to the kitchen, a huge room with every conceivable appliance on the worktops. Gavin identified some but not all of them—rice cooker, omelette maker, pizza maker, juicer, coffee machine, vegetable peeler.

"My mum likes to cook," said Marcia with a straight face.

On a table by the window were bowls of salad and cheeses, and bread and several nibbly things that Gavin did not recognize. The centerpiece was an enormous basket of fruit, also full of varieties he had not seen before.

Marcia fetched him a plate and they sat down at one end of the table. Gavin just had time to think that they must make a lonely picture, the two of them in this vast kitchen, when the arms of the chair grasped him round the chest and hauled him into an upright position.

Marcia giggled. "I forgot. It's BJ's posture chair. He's not allowed to slouch at the table. Do you want to move?"

"I'll cope," said Gavin. "We've got the earlier version at home."

"Have you?" said Marcia.

He nodded. "It's called Mum."

She laughed again and they helped themselves to food. Feeling that the atmosphere had thawed, Gavin ventured to ask, "Where's Boadicea?"

"I don't know. With the others, I expect. I told you, they've all gone." This time Marcia sounded annoyed rather than frightened.

"Gone?" He felt a tightening in his stomach.

Marcia shrugged. "Boadicea walked me home and I went upstairs and when I came down she wasn't here. I called next door and their robot's gone too. It's happened before. They don't disappear for long."

"But where do they go? Scuba diving?"

Marcia did not look amused. He said quickly, "Aren't you worried about what they might do? I mean, Boadicea scared you this morning. . . ."

"It was nothing. You just don't understand how modern robots work. They don't need batteries anymore, they get their power through radio transmission."

"You mean radio waves, like Eager does."

Marcia carried on as if he hadn't spoken. "There are radio transmitters all over the world now. Each type of robot has its own frequency and they simply tune in to the nearest transmitter."

"I understand," said Gavin. "But what has that got to do with Boadicea attacking you?"

"She didn't . . . !" Marcia's eyes flashed with temper. She made an effort to control herself and said deliberately, "I think this morning there must have been an interruption to the power. Boadicea probably had to switch quickly to another transmitter so she . . . she . . ."

"Fainted?"

He fancied that Marcia suppressed a smile. "Something like that," she said.

Gavin reached for an apple, although the knotted feeling in his stomach had grown worse and was spoiling his appetite. "That doesn't explain her behavior now. Or why the other robots have disappeared."

"I'm telling you, there's nothing to worry about. Dad says we must expect them to be unpredictable sometimes."

"Why?"

"Because the more a robot can think by itself the more com- plicated it becomes," said Marcia. "BDC4s aren't like Grumps, he's simple for a robot. You always know what he's up to."

He can spring a few surprises now that his timer's gone, thought Gavin, but he wasn't going to say that to Marcia. She went on, "Dad says LifeCorp's robots are the safest in the world. They won't harm us. Besides, the BDC4s are so intelli- gent that they like being friends with us. We just have to accept that they think for themselves."

Gavin thought of Eager. The robot was independent but he was also considerate. He couldn't imagine Eager walking off and leaving him with no explanation.

"Here, try some of this." Marcia was changing the subject by picking up the largest object in the fruit basket, a strange bulbous affair with orange-brown scales and spiky green fronds at one end.

"What is it?"

"A pineapple. Haven't you had one before?"

Gavin shook his head. "In that case," said Marcia, rising and going to a cupboard, "you must take it home for everyone to try." She dropped it into a carrier bag. "We've plenty here. There was a shipment last week."

Gavin thanked her and put the pineapple in his sports bag. "I'd better get back. Thanks for lunch."

As he walked down the hallway he noticed that the walls of the living room were now a restful green.

"Bye, Sir Gavin," said Marcia. "Watch out for dragons on the way."

Gavin blushed for the second time. Marcia surprised him by saying, "You don't mind my teasing you, do you? Only it's no fun teasing my own brother, he throws a tantrum."

Gavin bowed and waved his arm in a flourish. Imitating Grumps' gravelly voice, he said, "It's an honor, Lady Marcia."

Marcia laughed, and he felt self-conscious and ran off before she could say anything.

CHAPTER 13

Eager hurried down the slope, his excitement growing. The signals from the other robots were becoming stronger with each step: he must be close. Before long he would have a new circle of friends. Did Sphere know about this innermost wish of his? he wondered. Perhaps that was why it had sent him to the compound.

Halfway down the hill he came to an open space, where the turf was unusually green and lush for the time of year. A low building stood at the far end. Eager knew that he would find them there. He crossed the grass, feeling its dampness under his feet.

He could scarcely believe that he would soon be in the presence of these magnificent robots. As he drew near, the door of the building slid open and a dozen BDC4s stepped out, two abreast. Even in the faint sunlight their metals were dazzling. They appeared so purposeful and strong that Eager shrank back against the wall. This was not what he had intended to do, but by the time he summoned his courage and shouted, "Wait!" they were striding across the grass.

Eager watched them, fascinated. They kept together, walking with identical paces to the same rhythm. Step, step, step, step, step, step. When they reached the path they turned sharply to the right and went down the hill. They had not noticed him or, if they had, they showed no sign of it.

Eager ran across the field, his toes pulling at the grass, not stopping until he was halfway up the slope again. Above him rose a huge fluffy ball of pink blossom. The tree was the loveliest thing he had seen all day. He gazed up at it, feeling something of the awe that he had for the robots. Unlike the BDC4s, the tree seemed to be accepting of him. If only it could talk and move! He remembered the conversation with Fleur in the garden, and realized that he too was lonely.

* * * * *

Gavin stood at the gate, waiting for Eager. He looked at the jumble of different styles of houses and felt glad that he was not a technobrat. The compound struck him as an unfriendly place.

A glint caught his eye. Something bright was coming down the hill toward him. He squinted to bring it into focus, but there was no telling what it might be. Only as it came closer did he see a group of robots. One in the front row looked like Boadicea.

Gavin froze.

He told himself not to be such a moonrock, but there was

something disturbing about the robots. They were marching, staring straight ahead. Their tight formation gave them the invincibility of a tank. But the oddest thing about them was the fact that they were together at all. The BDC4s weren't built like robotinas or miners to work as teams. Why had they chosen to gather like this?

He noticed a large control box at the gate that he could crouch behind. It did not hide him completely: they would see him when they approached. He wondered what they might do to him, and tried to block out the image of Boadicea wielding the metal box. With luck, they might walk by . . . He peeped round just in time to see them veer off the path toward a row of cottages.

Gavin had been growing impatient to see Eager but now he was relieved that the robot did not arrive to attract the BDC4s' attention. Five minutes later he reassured himself that the robots were not coming back and began to feel cross with Eager. He did not want to miss the afternoon lessons as well, let alone the game of liveball. He checked that the hot fence was still turned off and walked through. Eager would have to catch him up.

It was such a relief to be free of the quarter that he hung his sports bag over his shoulder and broke into a small run. He jogged along, the bag with the pineapple in it knocking rhythmically against his back.

He was totally unprepared for what happened next. A hard object struck his outstretched leg and he stumbled, half falling, half pushed, face downward onto the pavement. He felt a weight on top of him, preventing him from rising, and hands began to rifle through his pockets. Someone lifted his arm and unclasped his jinn. His bag was wrenched off his shoulder. From the corner of his eye he could see the contents being thrown onto the ground. The carrier bag with the pineapple rolled toward the curb.

Gavin gasped for breath under the weight. He let out a groan and the heaviness lifted a little. A voice grated in his ear: "Come out exploring without your robot, have you? That was brave."

"Waste of time," said a ponderous voice. "This jinn is two years old. Rubbish."

Gavin struggled to free himself. He knew the attempt was useless but it made him feel better. "Who spliced *your* genes?" he said as scornfully as he could.

Surprisingly, the weight shifted and he was able to twist round and face his assailants, though they kept hold of his arms. They were boys, older than him, but not yet young men. The one sitting on him had a lean face. The other, who was holding Gavin's jinn, was short and thickset. He scowled at Gavin. The first boy looked almost amused. "You're not a technobrat," he stated.

Gavin shook his head. His mouth was so dry that he didn't trust himself to speak.

"Perhaps he's clever," droned the stocky boy. "Left his new matter at home."

They stared at him expectantly. Gavin swallowed. "What new matter?" he managed.

"New technology," the boy spat at him. "What else?"

Gavin looked uncomprehendingly at them. "I don't have anything else."

The boys exchanged glances. So, Gavin thought, these are marauders. To hear people talk about them, or rather, not talk about them, you would have thought they were three-headed monsters, not just boys.

A signal must have passed between them. The taller boy pushed Gavin back to the ground, snatched the sports bag and ran off, while his accomplice threw the jinn into the road and followed him. They didn't get far. Two lengths of rubber tubing shot out from behind Gavin and somehow grasped the boys by their wrists. Each tube began to wind in on itself, like a boa constrictor enfolding its prey.

Gavin swung round. "Eager!" he panted, more relieved to see a robot than he'd ever been before. It was the second time that day Eager had come to his rescue.

Gavin gathered up his sports kit and the pineapple, then doubled back to pick up the jinn. The marauders were digging their heels into the ground, trying to resist Eager's strength. It was no good. His rubber arms spun them round and round until their own arms were pinioned to their sides.

"Are you all right, Gavin?" said Eager. Gavin nodded and the robot hung his head. "I'm sorry. I . . . forgot the time." He seemed unaware of the two boys wriggling in his clutches. The stocky one kicked out, pointlessly.

"What shall we do with them?" said Gavin.

The boys' squirming became stronger.

"Police!" said the lean-faced boy, staring in alarm over Gavin's shoulder. "Let us go, will you? We haven't harmed you."

Gavin looked round and saw a burly police robot marching toward them. Everyone knew that the quarter was heavily patrolled but this was the first he had seen of it. The robot was too far off to have recorded anything, though there was no knowing how much he had witnessed.

"Please," urged the boy. "You don't know the trouble we'll be in. Not only us . . . We're not after money, just information. We need to know . . ." He didn't finish. The hefty robot was looking sternly down at them.

"Are you harmed, sir?" he asked Gavin. "I saw them attack you."

There was a flicker from the miniature camera between his eyes and Gavin realized that he was filming them. This made him even more nervous about taking a gamble. "I'm not hurt," he said, "because they weren't attacking me. We were just larking about. Playing around."

"Playing around," repeated the robot doubtfully. "That's what friends do."

"Exactly," said Gavin. "These are my friends." He could see from the corner of his eye that the marauders were holding their breath. Eager uncurled his arms to free them and they stepped forward, hardly able to hide their disbelief.

"Just a moment," said the police robot. "I am trained to recognize an attack when I see one."

Gavin knew that this was his chance to change his story. He caught the taller boy's eye, expecting to see despair or pleading. But the marauder looked at him calmly now, as if to say, "It's up to you."

"They were a bit rough but I . . . I was running away, you see, and things got out of hand. There's a pineapple in my bag and . . . I wouldn't show it to them. That's how it started."

The robot raised his eyes to the sky. "I've called my superiors. You will have to explain to them."

Gavin shrugged helplessly at the boys. They understood what the gesture meant. Human policemen would test them on each other's names and addresses and all those things that friends should know. It would be hard to sustain Gavin's story.

Eager stepped forward. "Am I a robot?" he asked.

"Yes," said the police robot.

"Do robots lie?"

"No."

"Then if I say that the boy is telling the truth you must believe me?"

"Yes."

"The boy is telling the truth," said Eager.

A flying pod swooped down and hovered above the pavement. A policewoman stepped out, followed by a man in plain clothes. "Well done, P7," said the latter to the robot.

He looked at the three boys, noticed a graze on Gavin's face and nodded toward the marauders. "Are these the boys?"

"I'm afraid I've made a mistake, sir."

"What mistake, P7?" said the policeman.

"I mistook their play activities for an attack. They are friends, sir."

The man cast a knowing glance over the group. His eyes did a double take when he noticed Eager but he quickly recovered himself. "Is this true?" he asked Gavin. "You seem to be hurt."

Gavin felt the side of his face. "Just a scratch. They didn't mean it. We were messing about."

"Sorry, Gav," said the tall boy.

Gavin was startled until he remembered that Eager had used his name. He hated being called Gav, but he smiled as if they were old buddies. "'S all right."

"We'd better be going, then. Are you sure about this, P7?"

"Yes, sir."

The policewoman leant forward and said in a low voice, "He's due for a yearly service, sir."

"Is that so?" said the policeman. "Well, boys, if you ever do need us, you can see how quickly we respond. The same is true, of course, if you ever think of misbehaving." He beamed at them and they raised a smile in return.

P7 followed the police officers into the back of the pod and the three of them took off.

CHAPTER 14

With the police officers gone, Gavin began to think that he had been foolish. He was not afraid of being attacked now that Eager was there, but he was cross that the marauders were getting off scot-free. On top of that he felt awkward with them. After all the playacting of being friends the boys were still strangers, and hostile ones at that.

While he wondered what to say, Eager burst out, "If you'll pardon my saying so, there's no virtue in attacking people, especially someone younger and shorter than you."

The stocky boy said, "We was just doing our job."

The lean-faced boy looked amused again. "You're not a LifeCorp robot, are you? Where're you from?"

Before Eager could reply, Gavin said loftily, "An independent manufacturer." He had drawn courage from Eager's forcefulness and added, "Aren't you going to explain? I hope I got you off for a good reason."

Nearby a hoverbus hummed. A woman came out of an office building and crossed the road. Otherwise the street was empty.

The boy held out his hand. "Errol," he said. "And that's Srin." Gavin shook hands, albeit cautiously.

"We're sorry, of course," said Errol.

Gavin wondered what the "of course" might mean. If people who went round mugging others were sorry, why did they do it?

As if he had read Gavin's thoughts the older boy continued, "We have to do it if we're to find out anything. We try not to hurt anyone. Just trawl."

"Trawl?"

"Take what we need. Technology."

"But what for?" said Gavin. "Someone else's jinn would be no use to you, you couldn't break the encryption."

He noticed for the first time that Errol's eyes were surprisingly candid.

"We don't use the jinns, we don't trust the gobey network anyway. Whatever we find we bring to our own scientists. They take it to pieces to see what the technocrats are doing. That way we keep up with their technology."

"Couldn't you just buy one . . . ?" The moment he opened his mouth Gavin recognized that this was a stupid question. "I suppose you can't afford it," he said lamely. "But why do you need to keep up with the technocrats?"

"One day they might use their technology against us," said Errol. "And we won't stand a chance."

"Why would they do that?" gasped Gavin. "You make it sound like a war!"

"It is," said Srin.

Errol shot him a warning look. "You don't know much, do you?" he said to Gavin. "Everything's hunky-dory far as you're concerned."

Gavin was not sure how to respond. It was true that his family was much better off than the city people. On the other hand, there were so many things he was prevented from doing. . . . "I suppose it is," he said. "Life's good."

To his surprise, Errol laughed. "We can all say that. After all, no one's starving or homeless these days. Not here, at any rate. But there are still things we need to fight for." He broke off.

"What sort of things?"

For the first time there was passion in Errol's eyes. "Freedom. The freedom to do and say what we want, to travel and live where we want, to choose our own jobs, to build things for ourselves . . ."

Gavin found himself nodding in agreement. "It's the same for us. We can't go abroad, and I'll have to do the same job as my dad, or some other profession . . . I can't be a scientist or an engineer, or . . . a musician!"

"Yep," said Errol, nodding in turn. "And even if you was a technobrat, you'd still need a license from the government to do engineering or science. And who do you think gets most of the licenses? The technocrats who work for LifeCorp."

Gavin was surprised at his tone. "Well, it is the biggest and best company in the world," he said.

Errol sneered. "Ever stopped to think why?" He did not wait for an answer. "Because LifeCorp makes the technology that the government needs to control us. That's why we don't trust the gobetween. LifeCorp built it and the government uses it to keep track of us."

It took Gavin a moment to take this in. LifeCorp and the government were working together! Though no one had said as much to him before he must have half known it for some time, from things he had overheard adults say. Nevertheless, after his many sessions with the philosopher, he liked to reason for himself.

"LifeCorp isn't the only business in the world," he argued. "We buy things from lots of other companies. They must have licenses too."

"Even LifeCorp can't run everything," said Errol.

"Doesn't stop 'em trying," growled Srin.

"And haven't you noticed how small these other companies are?" said Errol. "LifeCorp don't like real competition. Take your robot here. . . ." He jabbed a finger at Eager. "What do you think would happen if your 'independent manufacturer' wanted to build hundreds of robots like this one—assuming he has a license, of course?" He winked at Gavin. "I don't think LifeCorp would be very pleased, do you?"

Snippets of the conversation at the professor's house floated back to Gavin: "Commercially sensitive . . . think carefully how to launch Eager on the world . . ." These words had puzzled Gavin at the time, but what if the professor had been referring to LifeCorp?

Srin half punched Errol in the arm. "We been here too long, 'Rol. Another patrol will come."

"Wait!" said Gavin. "You aren't really going to fight LifeCorp and the government, are you? I mean, how can you?"

"Not on our own, perhaps," said Errol. "But other scientists are joining us even technocrats—'cos they don't like what LifeCorp is up to."

"What exactly are they doing?" said Gavin.

"Errol!" pleaded Srin.

The lean boy brushed him off. "OK, OK!"

As he moved away Errol noticed Gavin's tight-lipped expression. "Are you angry, Gav?"

"My name's Gavin," he said in a surly voice. He was remembering the moment when he lay captive on the ground.

Errol said something quietly to Srin, who stepped toward Gavin, his hands in front of his chest, palms outward. "C'mon, then."

Before he knew what he was doing Gavin had lunged forward and was pounding Srin's hands with his fists. Furiously he struck the wide fleshy palms, while Srin moved back and forth to absorb the shock. Eager looked on, wondering what the strange ritual might mean. Eventually the fight went out of Gavin. He dropped his arms and stood with head bowed, panting slightly. He felt his hair being ruffled and heard Errol's laugh.

"Well done, kid." Errol glanced at Eager, who was standing a few paces off. He held his gaze for a moment, then turned and caught up with Srin.

"What are you going to do now, Gavin?" asked Eager. The boy was staring at the pavement and the robot hoped to stir him into action. Gavin did not move.

There was a chirping noise and a voice said, "Omar calling."

Gavin gathered his thoughts. "Omar," he said, relieved to know that his jinn was still working. "Sorry, I'm not going to make the game. Um . . . something came up. Will you apologize for me? Thanks."

"I'm sorry," said Eager when the call had finished. "Your day is ruined and it's all my fault."

Gavin had not believed that a robot could look so forlorn. He wanted to laugh but thought that Eager might be offended.

"No, it isn't. Everyone's late sometimes. It might sound strange, but I'm glad I met the marauders, even if it hurt a bit." He grinned. "Besides, you rescued me. . . . That reminds me, you lied just now—you only pretended to tell the truth to the police robot."

Eager nodded. "I can choose how to behave, as you know. I try to choose not to lie, but it isn't that easy, I find."

"It certainly isn't," said Gavin.

The robot still looked crestfallen. "At the girl's house, I

didn't tell you the whole truth. I went to explore because I was picking up a different radio frequency. I wanted to meet the BDC4s."

Gavin's stomach clenched as he recalled the marching robots. "And did you?"

Eager hesitated. "Not really."

"Just as well," muttered Gavin. "Listen, don't tell anyone about this afternoon. If Mum or Dad ask about my face, I did it playing liveball." He looked intently at the robot. "Perhaps a couple more lies won't matter in the circumstances, if you don't mind?"

"Not at all," said Eager solemnly. "In the circumstances."

CHAPTER 15

Back home, Eager went to the kitchen to help Grumps. Gavin caught up on the classes he had missed that afternoon. An expert teacher on the gobetween took him through the lessons. It was satisfying to have all his questions answered, though he was sorry not to have worked with his friends at the learning center.

He came out of the study to the tantalizing smell of Grumps' shepherd's pie, and hurried upstairs to the top of the house. "Get me Socrates," he said, reaching for a pair of glasses.

The screen conjured up the philosopher under the tree and the buildings in the background. The time must be late afternoon, for the sun was declining. Gavin sat down on the grass.

"I've got a question," he said. "Do you remember I explained to you about robots?"

The philosopher inclined his head.

"And I wondered what would happen if we built one with free will? Well, we've got a new robot just like that. Professor

Ogden, who built him, said he wasn't programmed how to behave. I didn't really believe it. Now I do."

"What is your question?" said Socrates with a backward glance at the setting sun. "I shall have to go soon to get ready for dinner."

The remark gave Gavin an idea. "Who's preparing your dinner, Socrates?"

The man frowned. "Why, my slaves, of course."

"We don't have slaves," said Gavin, "we use robots to work for us. Nobody minds because robots don't get bored and they never complain about doing the same old things over and over again."

"Are they not slaves nonetheless?"

"No," said Gavin firmly, "because they're machines. There's nothing else they want to do. Whereas I bet your slaves would love to pop down to the beach or the river or . . ." He tried to think of ancient Greek pastimes. ". . . or talk philosophy."

"Indeed, I have been known to discuss it with them," said Socrates unexpectedly. "Their understanding is as good as that of many citizens I can think of."

"But not good enough for you to set them free?"

Socrates looked shocked at the proposal. Gavin said hastily, "I don't want to get into an argument because times have changed. The point is, although we don't believe in slavery, we expect robots like Eager to do all the work for us. But Eager is different to other robots."

"If this Eager is a machine, is it not logical to expect him to do as the other machines?"

"He is a machine, but he doesn't do things in a machinelike way."

"This is beginning to sound like a riddle," said the philosopher, sounding unusually irritable.

Gavin agreed. The discussion was going round in circles and he was unsure how to break the cycle.

"I've got to go for my dinner too," he said. He stood up. "I hope your slaves cook as well as mine." But the joke did nothing to lift his spirits.

* * * * *

In the living room his parents were drinking wine from tall glasses. It was unlikely to be champagne, which cost a lot because it had to be transported from France. Yet it was sparkling and they seemed in a party mood. Gavin was glad that someone had had a good day. He sank down on a floor cushion, angling himself to keep his grazed cheek from view.

"What are you celebrating?" asked Fleur, who had followed her brother into the room.

"I don't expect you'll be interested," said Mr. Bell in a tone that suggested the opposite. "I've just been given a crack team of BDC4s to work for me. I've never known robots with such common sense. Usually I have to explain things two or three times in different ways. These BDC4s hear an instruction and fly with it. You would think they'd lived and worked in buildings for years."

His children looked stony-faced. "Well, that went down well," he said. "Just the other day, Fleur, you were clamoring for us to buy one. If only we could."

"That's before I'd met one," she said.

"Are you disillusioned too?" his father asked Gavin.

"I don't trust them," Gavin said.

"Don't trust them?"

"And if they're so clever," Gavin went on, "maybe they shouldn't be building factories. What if they want to write poetry or play liveball?"

"An amusing idea . . . ," said Mr. Bell.

The green light by the door flickered. "There's a call for Fleur," said the house.

"Sarupa?" said Fleur, half rising.

"Marcia Morris."

Fleur sat back down. "Tell her I'm busy."

"My news must be boring too," said Mrs. Bell, "but never mind." Her husband leant across to refill her glass. "Cheers! I've just bought a team of BDC4s for the hotel. You know we have butlers in all the suites? Well, the new BDC4s are going to replace them as 'personal aides' and the butlers will be assigned to the other rooms. It's all part of our technology upgrade."

"Robots, robots, robots." Fleur stood up. "I'm going to talk to some real people."

"Charming," said her mum. "I suppose we're just holograms."

"I don't know why everyone is making such a fuss," said Fleur, turning in the doorway. "They're machines, that's all."

"Will it cheer you up to come to tea tomorrow?" said her mum. "It's the first day of our new Viennese pastry chef. He's famous for his strudel."

Gavin spluttered with laughter, and even his sister had to smile at the description. "OK, thanks," said Fleur. The door closed behind her.

"Dad," said Gavin, "do you remember what you said on the way to Professor Ogden's house? About the time you learned not to fight with a robot. What happened?"

"You've heard this before," Mr. Bell said to his wife.

"I don't mind," she said. She sipped her wine.

"It goes back to when I was a student architect. We had robot patrols that were programmed to lock up at night after checking that no one was left in the building. One evening I was working late, putting the finishing touches to a model. The glue was evil-smelling so I pushed the model on a trolley out into the corridor.

"Now, these robots were also programmed to keep the fire escapes in good condition and make sure the exits were clear. Suddenly I heard the sound of smashing wood. I rushed into the corridor to see one of the robots crushing my model to splinters. I yelled at him to stop, then grabbed his arm and struggled with him. I might have been a fly for all the notice he took. He flung me off with such force that I flew backward into the room and slammed into a table. I was bruised for weeks."

"Robots aren't supposed to harm us!" cried Gavin.

"But if they think we're going to cause harm, they can restrain us," said his dad. "This robot's main objective was to protect humans by keeping the fire exit clear. My model was in the way so he had to move it. I tried to stop him so I had to be stopped."

"All it had to do was ask you to move the trolley," protested Gavin.

"Those early robots didn't have much reasoning power, I'm afraid," said his dad.

"You don't know what a luxury it is nowadays not to have to think twice when you talk to a robot," said Mrs. Bell. "The misunderstandings we used to have . . ."

Gavin thought back to the events of the day. Perhaps Boadicea had a goal of her own that led her to threaten Marcia.

The green light by the door flashed on. "Supper is ready," said the house.

* * * * *

Fleur went to the room on the top floor. "There is a call for you from Marcia Morris," said the gobetween.

"I know," said Fleur.

"She's waiting."

Fleur closed her eyes and counted to five. "All right, I'll speak to her."

Marcia was in her bedroom sitting on a yellow gingham arm-chair that matched her bedspread. Her lap seemed to be full of iced biscuits. Fleur wondered absently why she didn't use a plate.

"Fleur!" she cried, moving so close to the camera that Fleur could see that her eyes were red and puffy. "You'll never guess what's happened!"

Fleur did not want to guess. Her attention went to the biscuits, which Marcia had begun to finger nervously. "My dad smashed my pot!" Marcia's voice wavered as she spoke. She held up what looked like a pink biscuit.

Fleur realized that it must be a shard from the pot and felt a stirring of compassion. "Was it an accident?"

Marcia shook her head and let out a cry. "He really liked it. He said how beautiful it was and I was so happy. I told him I wanted to be an artist when I grow up and he got angry. And then . . . and then . . . he just swept the pot off the table and . . ." The rest was lost in sobs.

"Oh, Marcie, I'm so sorry."

"We're still friends, aren't we? I'm really sorry about what I did."

Fleur chewed her lip. On the whole Marcia wasn't that bad a friend. She couldn't help acting like a technobrat sometimes. "That's OK."

Marcia was wiping her eyes with her sleeve.

"I don't understand what's wrong with being an artist," said Fleur encouragingly. "Lots of Mum and Dad's friends are artists and they do all right."

"They won't let me live here if I'm an artist," said Marcia. "Only technocrats and government officials—you know that."

"But surely—"

"I could marry a technocrat, of course, but I might not. I'd have to leave."

Fleur thought about the artists she knew. Obviously they were poorer than Marcia's family and friends, but somehow they seemed a lot happier. Now that she thought about it, Marcia's parents were almost always bad-tempered, even when they were supposed to be relaxing.

"There are other nice places to live. There's a whole community of artists in the city—"

"Are you stupid?" snapped Marcia. "Live with marauders and sweep the streets in my free time?"

Fleur fumed. Marcia hadn't changed a bit. "Why don't you talk to that robot instead of me? I'm sure Boadicea will know exactly what to say."

To her surprise Marcia's face crumpled. Fleur had never seen her look so vulnerable. "I don't trust her, Fleur. I thought she was wonderful but she wanders off and sometimes I think she's laughing at me. I've caught her watching in a sly way, as if she's scheming. . . ."

"Have you told your dad?" Fleur thought it was a futile question as she spoke, but she couldn't think of anything better to say.

"You know Dad—all technology is wonderful and LifeCorp is the greatest company in the world and I should be downright grateful to have the very latest robot before anyone else."

Fleur could imagine Mr. Morris saying this. The sympathy she had felt for her friend resurfaced. "Shall we meet tomorrow? We could have a history class together."

Marcia's face was wan. She nodded weakly. "I'll try." Before Fleur could ask her what she meant, she gestured to the gobetween to switch off.

Fleur found herself staring at a cascade of virtual rose petals. "Get me Chike in Nigeria," she said.

With her many gobepals scattered across the world, Fleur had become an expert in time zones. She knew exactly who would be in bed or studying at any given time. As she had guessed, Chike was in his studio.

"Hi, Fleur." He grinned and continued to beat softly on a small drum. "This is background music for my new recording. And I'm playing this." He brandished an oboe at her. "But it's not ready yet, you can't hear it. How are you?"

"Fine," she said.

He beat an angry-sounding rhythm on the drum. "You look fed up to me."

She sat on the floor and clasped her hands around her knees. "Have you seen the new range of BDCs?"

Chike stopped playing. "The BDC4s? LifeCorp is using them at the oil fields here. But only technocrats can buy them."

"I know," said Fleur. She waited. His expression had not changed but somehow she knew that he had more to tell her.

"People here say . . ." He stopped. "You'll think we're mad, superstitious," he said, shaking his head dismissively.

"No, I won't," said Fleur. Of all her gobepals he was one of the most thoughtful, and she trusted his judgment.

"They say there's something wrong, unnatural, about them."

"Unnatural?"

He shrugged. "I expect some people said the same thing about hoverbuses when they first saw them. You cannot take it seriously."

"Then why are you telling me this?"

Chike laughed and played a triumphant drumroll.

Fleur realized that he was not going to tell her any more. "I'll leave you to finish recording," she said, "but will you do me a favor? If you hear anything else about the BDC4s, let me know?"

"I will," he promised, and beat her a loud farewell.

CHAPTER 16

Fleur was in a rowing boat on the ocean, sailing away across a tranquil sea, the sun making emerald patterns on the water. She was with Marcia, they were friends again, and Marcia had promised to take her to a land where she could have everything she wanted. The boat began to rock. She gripped hold of the sides and tried to steady it. The rocking grew worse. . . .

"Fleur! Wake up." Gavin was shaking her.

She knew without opening her eyes that it was pitch dark.

" 'S the middle of the night. . . ."

"I need to talk to you."

Fleur raised an eyelid and shut it quickly against the light coming from the half-open door. She curled herself tighter into a ball and nestled into the pillow. If she only kept her eyes closed and stopped her mind from thinking she could let Gavin talk and as soon as he finished she could drift back to her deep sleep. . . .

"Fleur!"

"What?" she groaned.

"I need to talk to you. It's about the BDC4s, there's something strange about them . . ." He sat down at the end of her bed.

She forced herself to make an effort. "You woke me up to tell me that? I was having the best dream ever. . . ."

"Everyone seems to think they're euphoric and I'm beginning to wonder if I'm going mad because I'm the only one who doesn't. But you don't agree, do you?"

She wriggled out from under the duvet. "Have you just been playing a gobegame? All those monsters and crazy characters . . ."

"No, I haven't. I know I'm talking about real life. Listen, Boadicea nearly hit Marcia today."

"What!" Fleur was awake now. She sat upright and looked at him, wide-eyed with curiosity. Gavin told her what had happened at the learning center.

"Marcia said it was probably a power failure but I'm not convinced. I followed Marcia home—"

There was another exclamation from Fleur. Gavin went on, "Boadicea had just gone off and so had the other BDC4s. Marcia said it's because they're so intelligent—it makes them unpredictable. But I saw them later and they were like an army, marching together, eyes straight ahead. I don't know about unpredictable, it looked scary to me."

"No wonder she's frightened of Boadicea," said Fleur. Gavin looked questioningly at her. "I spoke to Marcia last night. I know I didn't want to but she wouldn't give up." She recounted what Marcia had told her.

"Scheming?" said Gavin. "Is that what she said? Well, I think all the BDC4s are up to something, not just Boadicea."

"And what would that be?"

"I don't know. Dad was talking about robots having some objectives that are more important than others. I think the BDC4s have got goals of their own. Why else would they wander off?"

"Since when were you an expert?" teased Fleur, though her own misgivings were almost as strong as Gavin's. "I spoke to Chike last night. He says people in Nigeria think the BDC4s are unnatural."

Gavin frowned. "What does he mean?"

"He wouldn't say or he didn't really know."

"Unnatural . . ." He pondered the word. "It's true they're not like any robots I know."

Fleur chewed her lip. "Perhaps we're just not used to robots being so humanlike."

"What about Eager? He's intelligent like us but he doesn't scare me. That's something else I don't understand. I thought Professor Ogden said Eager was the most advanced robot in the world, but these BDC4s seem to know much more than he does. So what did the professor mean? Was he wrong?"

Fleur interrupted. "How do they know so much?"

They eyed each other, grasping for thoughts beyond their reach. "Eager is learning from his experiences," said Gavin pensively. "You can see it happening. But I'm not sure about the BDC4s. It's as if—"

"They know everything already!" exclaimed Fleur. "But you can't program a robot to know everything. There's just too much information. And they don't only know things—they seem to understand, as well. I mean, Grumps can be taught to do tasks, but he doesn't understand why he should do them, or why they're important to us."

"Whereas Eager can understand too, but he has to be taught something first, like Grumps."

"Yes." Fleur went back to chewing her lip. "The BDC4s know *and* understand. But if they're not programmed like Grumps and they're not learning from experience like Eager . . ."

Gavin threw himself full-length onto the bed. "It's beyond me."

"We're not going to solve anything now," said Fleur, "so can I go back to bed?" A wave of irritability came over her as she thought of the sleep she'd lost. "I don't know why you had to wake me to talk about this now!"

"That's not the whole story. I'm sorry but—"

There were footsteps on the landing. "It's Eager," whispered Gavin, "going up to the gobey." They waited for him to pass.

"We'll need to talk to him later," said Gavin cryptically.

He sat up and noticed Fleur's irate expression. "Something else happened today," he added quickly. "Marauders attacked me."

"Marauders!"

"Shhh!"

He had expected her to be interested, though not to make such a fuss. She threw her arms around him and squeezed tightly. "My poor little brother! How dare they!" He managed at last to push her away. "No need for dramatics," he muttered. "I'm all right. They were quite friendly, actually."

"Omigod! Did you hurt your head?"

"I'm not concussed."

"But what did they do to you?" she gabbled, at once horrified and fascinated.

"I keep telling you, nothing. If you'll calm down, I can go on."

Squeezing the pillow between her shoulder blades and the wall, she sat back and looked at him earnestly. He described how the boys had ambushed him and Eager had caught them.

"Hang on, what was Eager doing there?"

He had hoped that she wouldn't ask. "I'll explain later, it's not important for now. A police robot came and I said we were just messing about—"

"What for?" shrieked Fleur. He shushed her again. "Did they threaten you?"

Gavin shook his head. "I can't explain why I did it. But I'm glad; otherwise I'd never have talked with them. Anyway, Eager put on this innocent face and backed me up so the police went away."

Fleur drew her knees to her chest. "I think you were temporarily deranged."

"They only attacked me because they thought I was a technobrat. They wanted my jinn or some other technology. Errol says it doesn't matter what they steal so long as it's new; then their own scientists can take it apart—"

"Errol?" said Fleur archly.

"I told you, we talked afterward. They introduced themselves."

"I can think of better ways to meet new friends," said Fleur.

Gavin couldn't help grinning. She had a point.

"So why do they want to steal jinns? And who are these scientists?"

"I don't know exactly," said Gavin. "They must be city scientists. But Errol says technocrats from LifeCorp are joining them because they don't like what the corporation's doing. They're in a sort of race to keep up with LifeCorp's technology in case they use it against them."

Fleur began to tap her chin against her knees. Like a demented magpie, Gavin thought. "Well, I don't get it. What is LifeCorp doing that's so bad? And what does this have to do with the BDC4s? If anything?"

Gavin admitted that he didn't know. "That's where my plan comes in. . . ."

"Which plan would that be?"

"I wish you'd take this seriously!" He rounded on her.

Fleur threw up her arms. "My younger brother's been attacked, Marcia's terrified of her new robot, BDC4s are marching about the place . . . of course I'm taking this seriously! But I don't really think there's much we can do about it."

"My plan," said Gavin slowly, "is just to find out more. We're going to Mum's hotel tomorrow. We can investigate the new BDC4s there, see whether they're like Boadicea and the others. Perhaps discover what their goals are."

"Do you really think Mum will let us wander about the hotel?"

Gavin looked steadily at his sister. "Not us, Fleur. Eager."

"Eager?"

"No one will be suspicious of a robot wandering around. They'll think he's staff. And the BDC4s might talk to him."

They heard footsteps, coming downstairs this time.

"We can ask him now," said Gavin, leaping up from the bed.

"Wait," said Fleur, "there's something you should know. I don't think the same about Eager as you do. I don't think he's any different from other robots, just a bit cleverer, perhaps."

Gavin paused in the doorway. "I see. But we could still ask him."

"Oh, yes," said his sister, "go ahead."

Eager had noticed the half-open door and was creeping past when Gavin called him. The family, unlike Professor Ogden, did not normally talk to him in the middle of the night. It surprised him even more to be beckoned into Fleur's bedroom. Full of curiosity, he stepped inside.

CHAPTER 17

At breakfast Grumps presented the family with the pineapple. It stood like an enormous jewel in the center of a silver tray.

"Where on earth did that come from?" said Mrs. Bell.

"I believe it originated in the Caribbean," replied Grumps.

"That's right," said Mr. Bell. "Must cost a fortune to transport them here. Coffee and tea are expensive enough."

"I haven't tasted one for years," said his wife. "The children probably don't even know what it is."

"A pineapple," said Fleur promptly, though she had never seen one in the flesh. She reached out to lift it up. "It's heavy!"

"I thought you would appreciate seeing it whole," said Grumps. "Shall I cut it now?" He sliced off the top and bottom and began to cut away the hard covering.

"Fancy remembering how to do it," said Mrs. Bell.

"But how did it come to the house, Grumps?" asked her husband.

"Master Gavin brought it."

All eyes, except Charlotte's, swiveled to look at Gavin. "Someone gave it to me at the . . . er . . . learning center. It was left over from . . . something, and this technobrat thought I might like to try it." Although his version was not far from the truth, Gavin felt himself blushing. He wished that he could lie as readily as Fleur, or even Eager, for that matter.

Fleur, who guessed the truth, raised her eyebrows at him.

"Generous friend," said their dad, popping a forkful of the fruit into his mouth. "Mmm, delicious. If he . . . or she, offers you anything else, I hope you say yes."

Gavin was relishing the sweet juiciness of the fruit and managed not to blush this time.

"I'll have some this evening," said Mrs. Bell, rising. "I have to get Charlotte ready for the day care center. I'll meet you all in the hotel at four. Grumps can bring you there from the center."

"Mum," called Fleur, "what about Eager? Can't he come?"

"That's very thoughtful of you." Mrs. Bell looked speculatively at her daughter. "Didn't you refuse to be seen with him in public?"

"Good idea, Fleur," said Mr. Bell. "We did promise to broaden his horizons."

"Thanks," said Fleur, smiling angelically at her mum.

■　■　■　■　■

The hotel where Mrs. Bell worked was just outside the city. It was an old stone building with porticos, and iron balconies on each floor.

"I believe this is the hotel," Grumps said to the children and Eager. "However, I must confess that I am confused." He stopped at the immaculate green lawn leading up to the entrance. A gravel drive bisected it. On either side were circular beds of white flowers.

"You're right, Grumps," said Gavin. "It's just that the garden has changed. Mum says the entire hotel looks different since it's been redecorated."

The gravel posed a problem for Grumps' wheels until Gavin spotted a narrow path alongside the drive. "Marble," he said. "Perfect for you."

A silver robot stood to attention in front of the main door. Its torso was painted in alternate red and green squares like a medieval knight's tunic. As it glided along the marble path toward them they saw that it also had wheels. "Good afternoon. Can I help you?"

While the robot resembled Grumps in its design and precise way of speaking, it was clearly a far newer model. The wheels were more like skates and the robot had the air of being able to see in several directions at once.

"We're just here for tea," said Gavin.

"No bags, then?" said the robot. "Enjoy your visit."

They walked through the door and had an instant impression of unruffled opulence. The reception walls were pale gold, globes of light appeared to hang in midair, and flowers spilled over on every surface. Mr. Bell stood up from a velvet-covered armchair to greet them. A second robot with the red and green livery came forward.

"Can I help you?"

"We're meeting Mrs. Bell for tea," said Mr. Bell.

"Mrs. Bell, head of employment, human and robotic," reeled off the robot. "She awaits you in the dining room. Follow me."

The dining room, like the reception area, was an oasis of calm and luxury. The Bell party sat at a table laid with a crisp white tablecloth, shiny cutlery and flowers. A woman harpist playing in a corner could be heard above the subdued chatter. At the other end of the room a pair of sliding doors opened and closed with startling speed as robot waiters went to and from the kitchen.

Charlotte, sitting in a high chair between her mother and Grumps, clapped her hands in delight at seeing everyone again.

"What do you think of the decoration?" Mrs. Bell asked her husband. "The designers call it the new traditional."

Mr. Bell twisted round in his seat. "Very impressive. Though I think our firm would have done it differently. . . ."

"You think it's over the top," said Mrs. Bell. "But our guests expect a little splendor."

"It looks expensive," said Gavin. "Who can afford to stay here now?"

"The usual people—technocrats and visiting government officials."

Eager sat quietly, noting the surroundings. It was novel for him to be sitting at a table. People and objects looked different from that angle. Gazing at the circle of faces around him, he felt almost as if he were seeing the Bells for the first time. It was a shame that he would not be there for long. He turned his attention to the waiters. They were silver with black torsos. The BDC4s only worked on the top floor, Fleur had said.

The Bells chatted until a waiter brought them the menu and they began to discuss the food. Eager remembered that this was his cue.

"Mrs. Bell . . ."

She lowered her menu.

"Do you mind if I go into the garden while you are eating? I didn't get a proper view of it. . . ."

"I expect you want to look at the flowers," said Fleur hurriedly. "He's very keen on them, aren't you, Eager?"

"Yes," said Eager, assuming what he hoped was a flower lover's expression.

"Of course, then. Off you go."

Eager jumped down from his chair and darted into the corridor.

"I didn't realize he was so sensitive," said Mrs. Bell fondly.

■ ■ ■ ■ ■

Eager skirted the outside wall of the dining room. Beyond an archway at the far end was a door. Fleur had said that it would lead to the kitchen, which was the place to find a tray. According to Fleur, it was important to carry a tray so that anyone he met would think that he was busy. She called it a prop. The door slid open and, sure enough, there was a whole pile of silver props in the corner. He seized one and made for the door.

"Ah, there you are."

Eager hopped back into the room, clutching the tray to his chest. A thin man in a black suit stood waiting for him.

"At last, an extra pair of hands."

"I'm very sorry," said Eager, quickly checking his limbs, "but I'm afraid I've only got the one pair."

The man rolled his eyes. "Don't they program you with idioms anymore? Cutting costs, I suppose." He looked doubtfully at Eager and at the tray in particular. "Has Mrs. Bell sent you?"

Eager thought it was better to go along with things rather than try to explain about the tray. He pondered the difference between "sent" and "brought" and decided that it was not so very great. "Yes, she has," he said firmly.

"Then follow me, we need help plating up. You won't be needing that," the man added, pointing to the tray. Eager replaced it on top of the pile, regretfully. The man led Eager through the kitchen, talking as they went. "The dining room's packed this afternoon and it's the pastry chef's first day. . . ."

Eager barely heard. The only kitchen he knew was the Bells'—a calm, orderly place where Grumps chopped and stirred in his methodical way and the appliances silently awaited his instructions. This kitchen was hot and noisy and everything seemed to be happening at once. Machines were slicing or peeling or mixing at lightning speed as if in competition with each other. People darted from oven to table, shouting out mysterious orders: "Ten whites, stiff peaks," and "One egg, half sugar, cream to smooth." A robotic arm furiously dispensed eggs from a huge carton.

At a table stood a man in a white hat, rolling a large ball of dough. Since his arrival at the Bells' house Eager had learnt to give flour a wide berth, but he was fascinated by how deftly the man flattened the ball with the rolling pin. When it was a thin sheet, he slipped his hands underneath the dough and stretched it even more. Eager came closer and could see the man's knuckles through the almost translucent pastry. The man stepped sideways and bounced off Eager's rubber frame.

"*Gott in Himmel!* Out of my way!" he exclaimed.

Eager recovered his balance and leapt aside. The man took another step around the table, still moving his hands, and the sheet of dough seemed alive as its edges wriggled further and further apart.

"Come along, now," barked the thin man, hurrying to a serving hatch at the other end of the kitchen. A robot with a brown torso stood by a conveyor belt, arranging sandwiches on plates. The man glanced nervously at Eager. "Just stand at the end of the line and add the final garnish."

Before Eager could ask what a garnish was, and especially a

final one, the man strode off. "Hello," said Eager to the robot. "Could you tell me what a garnish is, please? It's not something Grumps has taught me."

"In the pots," said the robot, without turning round. There was a row of bowls beside the serving hatch. Eager peered in and found cucumber, lettuce, chopped nuts, carrots, watercress, tomatoes and herbs. A plate of sandwiches bobbed toward him on the conveyor belt. He carefully placed on top of the bread several slices of cucumber and tomato, some lettuce leaves, a sprig of parsley, and a carrot shaped like a rose.

"Be quick," urged a robot waiter on the other side of the hatch, and no sooner had Eager sprinkled nuts over the plate than the waiter seized it and hurried off.

The plates kept on coming. There was no time to place the garnish elegantly—Eager had to work at high speed just to get all the items on the plate. At last there was only one lot of sandwiches remaining. Eager looked round for a waiter.

"You'll have to serve them," said the brown robot. "Table twenty, left-hand corner."

Eager had been planning to slip away now that the garnishing was finished. But it was a small task, he told himself, and he would feel that he had done his duty. He picked up the plate.

He had forgotten about the doors to the dining room. They parted to let him through, then sprang shut so fiercely that he had to jump out of their way. He glared at them indignantly over his shoulder.

After the heat and chaos of the kitchen the dining room was like a distant country. He had to take care not to rush. Fortunately the Bells sat at the far end and might not see him. Table twenty was occupied by a man, a woman and a small girl. Eager proudly held out the plate of sandwiches.

"What's this rabbit food?" said the man. "Where are my sandwiches?"

"Underneath," said Eager politely.

"Underneath?" blustered the man. "When I order food I don't expect to have to dig for it."

Eager took a step backward under the force of the man's wrath.

"Don't get upset, dear," said the woman. "It's only a robot, it can't help it. Waiter, I would like an apple strudel. And so would my daughter. With cream."

"Certainly," said Eager.

"That's *two* apple strudels," said the man.

Eager gave him a cold look and went back to the kitchen. There was some sort of disturbance over by the serving hatch. A dozen robot waiters, each holding a lettuce-covered plate, jostled for space, while the man in the black suit waved his arms and shouted at them. Eager decided to assign himself a new job of fetching the apple strudels. He hurried in the opposite direction toward a large trolley of puddings, presided over by a thin robot with many arms.

"Two slices of strudel, please."

An arm with a chopper on the end rose and fell, rose and

fell. A hand like a palette knife nudged the slices of strudel onto plates. A third arm put them on a conveyor belt. "And cream," said Eager. The multiarmed robot did nothing.

"How many?" growled a squat machine with many nozzles as the first plate stopped beneath it.

Eager considered. Whenever the family had cream Mrs. Bell nearly always said to Gavin that one helping was plenty. "One," said Eager. The machine whirred and squeezed cream neatly onto the plate beside the strudel. Eager picked up the plate, and the second one took its place.

"How many?" repeated the machine.

A waiter approached and took the first plate of strudel from Eager. "Which table?" asked the robot.

"Twenty," said Eager.

With a whir, the machine spewed cream onto the second plate. Before Eager could pick it up the plate had rotated and a second dollop of cream was dropping onto the side. The plate turned again and a third dollop fell . . .

"*Stop!*" Eager shouted. "I wasn't talking to you. Stop!" But the machine continued its relentless dispensing. Eager bent over to catch the cream that was now toppling over the side of the plate. It was like clutching at water. "Stop! No more!" he cried.

He straightened up to find himself nose to nose with the man in the white hat. "*Gott in Himmel,* you again!" The man turned to the machine. "*Nein!*" he roared.

"Nine!" cried Eager. "That's a lot of cream for a small girl. Even Gavin would be sick."

The cream dispenser stopped dispensing and the pastry chef glowered at Eager. Eager stared back. The man was already red-faced from the heat of the kitchen but it seemed to Eager that he was turning crimson. "Are you all right?" the robot asked.

The pastry chef was having difficulty speaking. "This is a precision machine," he managed at last. "What have you done to it?"

"I don't know about precision," said Eager, "but it hasn't got much common sense. Fancy giving anyone twenty helpings. I think you should have a word with it," he added helpfully.

The pastry chef's jaw dropped open. Eager looked round for something to wipe the cream off his hands. There was a fine white towel on the table behind the machine and he picked it up. Too late, his fingers pierced the fabric and he realized that it was the strudel dough that the pastry chef had been carefully stretching. He stood there dripping stickiness from his fingers and observed the horror-struck face of the pastry chef bearing down on him.

Eager looked the other way and saw that there was still a commotion at the serving hatch and that the thin man was also coming in his direction. He tilted his head to consider his predicament. An instant later he had shot through the snapping doors and was racing across the dining room toward the Bells' table. He swerved just in time to escape through the archway.

CHAPTER 18

Eager took the lift to the top floor. By the time the door opened he had managed to rub away most of the cream and dough from his fingers. He stepped out onto the thickest carpet he had ever walked on. In fact, he could hardly walk on it at all, but had to raise his feet in an exaggerated way because the carpet tufts got caught between his toes. He wondered how other robots managed, then remembered that this was where the BDC4s worked. Their metal, shoelike feet would have no problem.

Eager was carefully lifting up a foot when a door along the corridor opened and a man in a bathrobe poked his head out.

"Where's Douglas?" he demanded.

Eager was so taken aback that he stood there with his foot in midair. "I've no idea," he said.

"What in heaven's name are you doing?"

The robot recognized a trap. The last time he had been in this situation he had ended up working in the kitchen. He would have to be very careful how he replied. He could not afford to be diverted from his mission a second time. "I'm looking for the BDC4s," he said boldly.

To his astonishment the man beckoned to him. "That's easy enough." He nodded toward the room next door. "They're in there. I keep popping out to look for Douglas and I've seen them go inside."

"All of them?" said Eager.

"About ten of them. It can't be all of them because Douglas is missing, for one. He took my clothes to be express cleaned," the man added irritably. "That was four hours ago. I don't call that express, do you?" Before Eager could reply he went on, "I expect you're wondering why I haven't called the manager to complain. It's only his first week and . . . I don't expect you to understand . . . but if he wasn't a robot I'd say he was a nice bloke."

Eager was finding it hard to follow the man. On top of that he was dumbfounded at being talked to in this way.

"The sort of fellow I'd have a drink with," continued the man. "So I thought I'd give him a second chance. Ridiculous, I know."

"What are they doing next door?" asked Eager without thinking, and immediately regretted the question. Fleur had explained that on no account was he to arouse suspicion by showing suspicion himself. But the man merely shrugged. "Why don't you go in and see?" he said. "And if Douglas has sneaked in, send him to me at once."

He turned to go back into the room. Eager walked along to

the room next door. All he had to do was knock. Now that the moment had come, what could he say to the BDC4s? What if they sent him away?

"I've had a better idea." The man had stuck his head round the door again. "Why don't you go the back way? Then you'll see them before they see you. Come on." Noticing the robot hesitating, he demanded, "Are you coming or aren't you?"

Eager followed him into a sitting room with a gobetween on one wall and doors along another, and through wide French windows onto a terrace. There were shrubs around the sides and a small fountain in the center. The early-evening sky was a vaporous gray.

"Just climb over here," said the man, indicating a wall between the terrace and the one next door. "I'd come too but there might be another guest in the room." He laughed. "You staff can get away with spying but I couldn't."

At the word "spying" Eager's system did an internal somersault. This was exactly the word that Fleur and Gavin had used. He had thought his job would be difficult, yet here was a stranger not only encouraging, but helping him. "Are you a friend of Fleur?" he asked.

The man looked curiously at him for a moment. "Fleur? No, I would remember a name like that." He smiled sheepishly. "You probably think my behavior is a bit odd. I'm not a technocrat but I've always been interested in science, you see. I suppose I've read too many stories about robots . . . most of them are just clever machines, I know. That's all you are, possibly. But these BDC4s intrigue me. What are they up to in there?" He glanced back at the partition.

"That's what *we* want to know," said Eager.

"Hurry up, then," said the man, as if he had only half heard Eager. "Do you need something to climb on?"

"No." The rubber rings of Eager's legs stretched like elastic until he was tall enough to step over the wall. From the corner of his eye he saw amazement on the man's face. He contracted his legs to their normal length and looked around. The next-door terrace was almost identical to the first one, and the glass doors into the sitting room were also open. He heard music— several instruments playing at once in penetrating bursts of sound, and above them a woman's voice singing to the fast rhythm.

Eager edged his way along the wall to the open door. He peered round as two BDC4s crossed in front of him. Eager sprang back; so did the robots, apparently without seeing him. He ventured another look. The robots reappeared and this time one of them spun round quickly before Eager had a chance to move. He froze. It must have spotted him. But the robot gave no sign that it had.

Both robots stepped aside again, giving Eager a view of the room. A titanium BDC4 lay full-length on a sofa, one arm hanging languidly over the side. Eager counted five more ro-bots at the other end of the room. They sat in chairs or perched on the arms, watching a huge gobetween on the wall.

Eager just had time to take in the scene before the two robots crossed the doorway again. He hastily withdrew. There seemed to be a pattern to their actions. He counted the beats of the music until the robots reappeared. One of them spun round twice. Eager saw a flash of silver as the other robot stretched out an arm to catch it by the hand.

"Change the music," called a voice.

"We like it," said one of the robots by the door. The singer's rhythm grew faster and so did the robots' movements. When they moved aside, Eager peeked around the door again.

Abruptly, the singing stopped. A different music began that reminded Eager of the harp in the dining room, but this was a continuous flow rather than the broken plucking of strings. He found himself caught up in the music, wondering where it would go next, straining with the player to create higher and higher notes—shriller than any birdsong that Eager had ever heard.

"We can't dance to this," he heard one of the robots complain.

A new melody took over and the instrument stopped playing. For a moment Eager was still bewitched. Then the spell was broken. A door opposite the gobetween opened and another BDC4 came into the room.

Instantly the robots on the sofa and chairs leapt up and thrust their fingertips against their foreheads. The dancers by the door did the same. The gesture puzzled Eager, but his attention was fixed on the new robot. It was wearing a bathrobe.

There was nothing unbecoming about the sight. The robot

was tall and bronze; the robe fitted it perfectly. Eager knew that humans wore bathrobes when they were wet, or when they wanted to cover themselves up before going to bed. A robot had no need to wear a robe of any kind. He considered these things in a second, but it was long enough for the BDC4 to turn its head and notice him. They held each other's gaze.

"We have a guest," said the robot. He had a deep commanding voice.

The other robots registered surprise, though they did not move.

"Stand at ease!" said the robot in the bathrobe. As rapidly as they had raised them, the robots dropped their hands to the side.

"Won't you come in?" the robot asked Eager.

Eager was too bewildered to speak. He came into the room. The robots by the door moved too, taking up position behind him. Eager's head tilted as he tried desperately to make sense of what he was seeing. He did not know any robots except Grumps, but he was sure that most robots did not behave like this. These robots were acting like people. His head bobbed up.

"Ah!" he cried. "I understand! You're curious to know what it's like to be human."

An expression like anger passed across the robots' faces. "What would you know about that?" asked the robot that had been lying on the sofa.

"I . . . I . . ." Eager stumbled to find the right words to over-come the robots' hostility. "I'm curious too. The Bells are al-ways saying that I ask a lot of questions. That's the family I live with. . . . But it's difficult to make sense of their world, isn't it? After all, they didn't build it for us, they built it for themselves. Professor Ogden told me that we robots are designed to fit in, but of course we never can completely, can we?"

The BDC4s said nothing. Although they continued to stare at him, Eager felt as he had done at the learning center when the golden robot ignored him. Yet he could not contain his admiration of them.

"I've been searching for you," he said excitedly. "When I go on errands in the professional quarter I imagine meeting you. That is the wrong place, I realize now."

Still no response. "I thought we might have a lot in com-mon and we could talk about things. . . ." He tailed off. Eager had been unsure how the BDC4s would greet him, but he'd expected a little more enthusiasm for a fellow robot. He had forgotten his manners in his excitement. Perhaps that was it. "Please excuse my rudeness. My name is Eager."

There was a pause before the robed BDC4 spoke again. "I'm Bradoc."

"How do you—"

"Sea Captain Bradoc," the robot continued. "I don't know what you really want but if you think you're like us"—he swept his gaze over the other robots—"you're very much mistaken.

175

We have nothing in common with a robot like you." He spoke the word "robot" in a strange way, almost as if it had nothing to do with him.

Confusion engulfed Eager. He couldn't stand the robots' stony-faced expressions any longer. He turned to leave. The robots by the door barred his way.

"Excuse me," he said with all the dignity he could summon.

He noticed them glancing over his shoulder at the bronze robot, which must have given them a signal, for without taking their eyes off Eager, they moved out of the way. Eager walked onto the terrace.

"Goodbye, Eager," said the bronze robot behind him.

■   ■   ■   ■   ■

It was growing dark and the man next door was not on his terrace. Eager went into the sitting room, activating the lights. There was no sign of the man. He was about to leave when a voice called loudly from behind one of the doors, "Douglas!"

Eager followed the sound. "I'm not—" He broke off as he saw that the man was lying in a bath twice the size of the one in the Bells' house. Wide steps led up to it. The water was bubbling perilously like a kettle about to come to the boil. Only the man's head was visible and the buffeting of the water threatened to submerge him any moment.

Eager bounded up the steps. He saw the man's horrified

look as he prepared to jump. "It's all right!" he cried. "I'm waterproof!"

"I don't care if you're biodegradable!" shouted the man. "Get out of my Jacuzzi!"

The man sounded so vehement that Eager tried to step back but the bathtub was surprisingly slippery. One moment his foot was on the edge, the next it had slid from under him and his whole body shot like a torpedo into the water. A split second before his head went under, a pair of metal arms hauled him out.

CHAPTER 19

The Bells had finished their tea and were getting ready to leave the dining room when a young man approached them. "Excuse me, Mrs. Bell, could I have a private word?"

"You can talk here," she said, smiling. "My family's used to the ups and downs of hotel life."

Nonetheless, the man glanced anxiously around the table before continuing in a hushed voice: "There's been a problem upstairs. One of the new robots . . ."

He stopped as if it was painful to say more.

"I'll come at once." Mrs. Bell stood up and addressed her family. "Sorry about this. Why don't you wait for me in reception?"

Gavin and Fleur exchanged an anxious yet knowing look. It was just what they had feared. People will have to take the threat of the BDC4s seriously now, thought Gavin.

They waited for some time in the reception area. Charlotte fell asleep in Grumps' arms and Mr. Bell picked up a lexiscreen to read the news.

Fleur whispered to Gavin, "Where do you think Eager is?" He shook his head; then a movement by the lift caught his eye.

"Omigod," said Fleur.

Mrs. Bell had come out of the lift, followed by the young man and Eager. It was an odd-looking Eager. Dark patches spread over his rubber and his face had lost its usual animation.

"Trouble," said Gavin under his breath, thinking that this was an understatement. Aloud he said, "What's happened, Mum?"

Mrs. Bell had a stern look that he associated with his worst childhood misdeeds. "I was relieved to discover that the robot running amok was not a member of staff," she said testily. "Imagine my embarrassment instead when I had to admit that it was our family robot."

"Running amok?" said Fleur.

"I don't believe it," said Gavin, but he couldn't suppress a fear that perhaps all robots had a tendency to frightening, erratic behavior.

"Do you still have a job?" said Mr. Bell lightly.

"By the skin of my teeth."

"But what did he do?" cried Fleur, looking at the robot as if she were seeing him for the first time.

"Where do you want me to begin?" said her mum. "Impersonating a waiter, causing havoc in the kitchen, attacking a guest in his bath . . ."

Throughout the list of crimes Eager's eyes had been

179

downcast, but now he raised his head spiritedly. "I didn't attack him. I was rescuing him," he corrected.

"Is the guest all right?" said Mr. Bell.

"Once he'd got over the shock. In fact, he was surprisingly good-natured about it. Thankfully his BDC4 came and pulled Eager out of the bath before he could do any damage." Mrs. Bell sighed. "Let's go home before anyone changes their mind and has Eager clapped in irons."

Ordinarily, Eager understood, it was very pleasant to be clapped, but from the tone of Mrs. Bell's voice she had something less agreeable in mind. "I should like to go home, please," he said hastily.

The family was no longer looking at him. Their gaze had shifted to a gray-haired man coming toward them from the lift. Fleur in particular stared with interest at his wire-rimmed glasses.

"Mr. Lobsang," said Mr. Bell, rising to shake hands.

"Good evening," said the man. "And your son is here too. Hello! We talked on the gobetween, remember? I said then your father was a great architect, and he is proving me right!"

The Tibetan man was so friendly that Gavin began to think he was wrong to be suspicious of him.

His father was introducing Mrs. Bell and Fleur. "And that's our youngest member with the butler," he said, indicating the baby sprawled across Grumps' lap.

"And this?" said Mr. Lobsang, pointing to Eager. "Who might you be?"

A sudden change in his expression acted like an alarm to Gavin. Though the Tibetan was smiling, his eyes had narrowed, so that each half of his face told a different story. Gavin remembered Errol's words: "LifeCorp doesn't like real competition."

Gavin held his breath, praying that Eager would not respond. The robot was indeed so dejected that he simply looked at the man with listless eyes.

"Dad, let's go," said Gavin in a low voice. His father shot him a look that told him not to be rude.

"Fascinating," Mr. Lobsang was saying, still staring at Eager. "One of Morelli's designs, of course. I recognize his trademark."

Gavin knew, though he couldn't be sure how, that this was a trick. If "Mr. Morelli" existed at all, it was not to build robots like Eager.

"Actually he was built by a friend of mine," said Mr. Bell. The moment Gavin was dreading had come. "Professor Ogden. Do you know him?"

This time there was no mistaking the look that darted across Mr. Lobsang's face. Gavin saw clearly a mixture of recognition and hostility. It quickly passed and the man was smiling again. "No, I don't believe I do. The scientific community is large. Perhaps you could tell me more about your robot sometime?" he added.

"Are you staying here?" asked Mrs. Bell.

"Yes, until the new factory is built. We are about to begin the first mass production of BDC4s. It's very exciting."

"Well, we'd better get Charlotte to bed," said Mr. Bell. "Have a good weekend."

"Thank you," said the man.

Gavin lagged behind the others and glanced over his shoulder to see Mr. Lobsang watching them, a displeased expression lingering on his face. Gavin waved, as if that were the reason why he had turned round. The Tibetan was not the only one who could pretend, he reflected.

■ ■ ■ ■ ■

Eager stood against the kitchen wall, his head slumped on his chest. The room, which had become cozy and familiar, now seemed drab and unwelcoming. He wondered if his zest for life would ever return. There was a squeaking noise. Eager looked up as the butler rolled past.

"Did you ever make a mistake, Grumps?" he said.

The elderly robot steered his head round to look at Eager. "Many times."

"Did you?" cried Eager. "What kind of mistakes?"

"I have no idea," said Grumps, continuing on his way.

"Wait a moment. You must remember."

Grumps stopped. "As I understand it, the nature of a mistake is not to repeat it."

"But aren't you programmed to do things right?"

"We robots cannot be programmed to know everything,"

intoned Grumps. "Therefore we must learn, and learning involves mistakes. The same is true for humans, I believe."

Eager considered this. He knew that Gavin and Fleur were expected to spend a lot of time learning about different subjects, but he had never thought that they might be expected to make mistakes.

"So what happened when you did something wrong?" he said.

"I was shown the correct way to proceed," said the butler. "And once I knew the correct procedure, the old behavior was erased from my memory."

"Did you ever feel remorse?" said Eager. This was the word the philosopher had used after Eager nearly harmed Charlotte.

"Remorse?"

"Never mind," said Eager.

The door slid open to let in Fleur and Gavin. Grumps trundled away to recharge his batteries, leaving Eager alone by the wall. Although Fleur was still determined not to treat him like a person, his woebegone expression touched her. "I'm so sorry," she cried involuntarily.

"It was our fault," said Gavin. "I'm sure you did your best. We'll just have to find some other way of getting to the BDC4s."

"But I met them," said Eager.

Gavin and Fleur looked disbelieving. "You did?" said Fleur.

"They were in the room next door to the man. They were acting"—he thought for a moment—"like guests."

The weight of this description led Fleur and Gavin to sit down at the kitchen table. Eager recounted what he had seen and the words of the bronze BDC4.

"I tried to talk with them," said Eager dejectedly, "to win their confidence as you told me to. But they were unfriendly."

"What could they be doing in the room together?" mused Gavin. "Besides partying?"

The green light by the door flickered. "Fleur, Gavin, your parents wish to speak to you in the living room," said the house.

"Royal summons," said Gavin grimly. "See you later, Eager."

The robot dropped his head again. "I shall turn down my power and rest," he said.

Gavin and Fleur expected their parents to be cross about the events at the hotel but were unprepared for what followed.

"We've been discussing Eager," said Mr. Bell, in a solemn voice, "and we've agreed that he's no longer to be trusted. Don't protest. We have to face facts. You heard what Professor Ogden said, Gavin. He isn't ready to go into the world, that's why he's with us."

"I think what the professor really meant was the world isn't ready for Eager," said Gavin.

"You can say that again," sighed his mum.

"I didn't mean it as a joke. Eager's different, he's special. . . ."

"That may be," said Mr. Bell. "The point is, we've seen today how unpredictable he is. We can't take the risk of leaving him with Charlotte or even letting him out of the house."

"That isn't fair," protested Fleur.

"We know you're fond of Eager, especially you, Gavin," said their mum. "I am too. But just look what happened at the hotel. . . ."

Gavin and Fleur exchanged a look and came to an understanding. "It wasn't his fault . . ."

"We told him to go undercover . . ."

". . . it was ours!"

". . . to spy on the BDC4s . . . ," they said at once.

"Hold on," said their dad. "What's all this?"

Gavin spoke first, describing the BDC4s' strange behavior at the technocrats' quarter and Boadicea's threatening action with the metal box.

"Marcie says she's scared of Boadicea," added Fleur.

They saw a quizzical look pass between their parents. "What do the Morrises say about this?" said Mr. Bell.

Fleur answered reluctantly, "They say there's no problem. But how do they know?"

"Calm down," said her dad. "LifeCorp wouldn't put the BDC4s on the market if they hadn't been tested for months . . . years, probably. People like the Morrises have had them in their homes for several weeks and no one's found anything to worry about. Apart from Marcia. From what I've seen of her she's an attention seeker. It isn't enough to have the latest robot, she's got to find some drama—"

"I saw her on the gobey, Dad," cried Fleur. "She was scared." Yet at the back of her mind, Fleur knew that her dad was partly right about her friend.

"I saw her looking scared in real life," said Gavin.

"Listen," said Mrs. Bell. "It was a BDC4 who pulled Eager out of that poor man's bath this afternoon."

"But the rest of them were messing about," said Gavin. "Eager said they were dancing in the room next door. And watching a movie on the gobey . . ."

Mrs. Bell laughed. "I've never heard such a thing. You know, they're like butlers. It's their job to check everything in the rooms—music system, gobetween . . ."

"One of them was wearing a bathrobe."

"Don't be absurd, Gavin."

"Our minds are made up," said Mr. Bell firmly. "I shall call Professor Ogden in the morning and ask his advice. In the meantime Eager is to stay at home and Grumps must supervise him at all times. Am I understood?"

Gavin cast his eyes defiantly at the floor and Fleur chewed her lip. Eventually they replied, "Yes, Dad."

CHAPTER 28

Since it was the weekend, the house let the family lie in. As soon as it saw that Fleur was awake, the green light by her bedroom door flickered.

"Good morning. There is a call for you from Nigeria."

"Chike," said Fleur, swinging her legs over the side of the bed. "Tell him I'm on my way."

She climbed to the top of the house, where Chike, in T-shirt and shorts, was waiting on the gobetween.

"Hello," he said. His face fell. "What's wrong? You still look fed up."

Fleur plopped into a chair. "My brother had a wetbrain idea to spy on some BDC4s. Now my mum and dad are really cross with us."

"That's why I'm calling," said her gobepal. "You asked me for any news about them. Remember I said they worked at the oil fields? Well, yesterday they took a manager hostage. . . ."

Fleur sat up straight in astonishment.

"Everything's fine now. LifeCorp switched off their power supply and took them back to the factory. I thought you might like to know."

"Thanks," said Fleur. "What went wrong with them?"

Chike pulled a face. "You expect LifeCorp to tell us? It was on the news and they said it was a technical fault. I'll let you know if I hear anything else."

They said goodbye and Fleur sat thoughtfully for a moment. "Gobey, get me Sarupa."

A minute or two passed. "She is not at home. I shall have to call her jinn." More seconds went by until Sarupa's face appeared.

"You're enormous!" shrieked Fleur. "Gobey, reduce the screen!"

The girls laughed together. "How's your robot?" said Fleur.

"Robot? You mean Badupca? Daddy sent her back to the factory. Nothing happened but he said there might be a problem, I don't know what. There's only twenty BDC4s in the whole of Bombay and they've all gone back for testing."

"Don't you miss her?" said Fleur.

Sarupa shrugged. "I thought I would. But I'm spending more time with my sister. Though Badupca didn't argue as much as she does!" They laughed again. "Do you want to come shopping with us this evening?' said Sarupa. "I've got new gobey glasses. . . ."

"I'd love to! But I'd better not. Mum and Dad are cross with me."

Sarupa made a sympathetic face. "Another time," she said. "Call me."

Fleur went downstairs to breakfast, thinking hard. It was scary if BDC4s were taking people hostage. On the other hand, Sarupa's robot had not done anything wrong, and apart from Gavin and Marcia no one else seemed to be worried. Fleur found Boadicea spooky, it was true, but perhaps that was because she was jealous of her. Fleur decided not to tell Gavin the news. He had a bee in his bonnet about the robots and it would only make him worse.

* * * * *

"How about a day trip?" suggested Mr. Bell at the breakfast table. Charlotte, excited by the tone of his voice, bounced up and down in her chair. His older children looked astounded. After the events of yesterday they hadn't expected to find him in high spirits.

"Your mum and I think we all need a break, something to cheer us up. It is springtime, after all. And perhaps . . . well . . . we wondered if we've been neglecting you both. We've been so busy recently, what with the new factory and the hotel being refitted."

Fleur stabbed at her cereal with her spoon. "How can we go anywhere?"

"Gavin told me he saw a petrol convoy the other day. He

was right, there are new supplies and I've managed to get hold of some. A delivery pod should be here any minute."

"Euphoric, Dad," mumbled Gavin, although that was the last thing he felt.

Fleur sounded more enthusiastic. "So where are we heading?"

"Out to the woodlands, for a good long walk. It's a bit of a dull day but the house says the weather should clear. We'll take Grumps too, to help with Charlotte if she gets tired."

Gavin could not stop himself asking, "What about Eager?"

There was an uncomfortable pause. "Gavin, you know what we said last night. He's not to leave the house."

"But if Grumps comes he'll be left on his own. Surely nothing can happen if he's with us?"

"We'll see what your mum says when she comes down. I don't suppose there's any harm in it. We could put Grumps in the boot to make room."

A loud bleeping came from the road. "Petrol," said Gavin, leaping up and going to the window. Half hidden by the lime tree was a small delivery pod, covered in hazard warnings.

Mrs. Bell came into the room. "Morning, everyone. Have you spoken to Professor Ogden?" she asked her husband.

He shook his head. "It's very odd. The gobey keeps saying he's inaccessible. I'll try again later. Let's get this petrol first. By the way, Gavin has suggested taking Eager rather than leave him on his own." He left the room and Mrs. Bell sat down.

"I don't see why not," she said wearily. "I've just spoken to

Eager and I've never seen a robot look so miserable, not even Grumps. He says he feels great remorse for causing so much trouble." She helped herself to toast. "A remorseful robot is more than I can bear. By all means, let's take his mind off things."

"Thanks, Mum." Gavin kissed her on the cheek as he ran out of the room.

He and Fleur went outside. Their father and Grumps were standing in the road beside the delivery pod. Mr. Bell held his hand against the pod's scanner so that it could read his palm print, and the domed roof slid back to reveal two cans of petrol. Grumps carried the cans to a garage at the side of the house, where he poured the viscous black fluid through a funnel into the car's petrol tank.

Fleur held her nose theatrically. "It stinks."

" 'Fraid so," said her dad. "You wouldn't believe it, but the petrol we used to get straight from the refinery smelt just as bad. OK, we're ready to load."

Getting Grumps into the boot was the trickiest part. In the end they told him to climb in and once he was lying down Mr. Bell removed his battery pack. Eager, who joined them at this point, found himself turning away. The sight reminded him of the dead robot in the back of the van outside the technocrats' quarter.

Then they remembered that Charlotte needed a car seat and that Grumps was the only one to know where it would be. Mrs. Bell disappeared into the house and was gone a long time before returning triumphant. It took several more minutes to fathom out how to interlock the car seat's old-fashioned straps.

Eventually Fleur and Gavin squeezed themselves into the back next to Charlotte and somehow made room for Eager, who sat half wedged between the front and back seats.

"This is no fun for Eager," said Gavin. "It's his first time and he won't be able to see anything."

"We all want to see out," remarked Fleur. "It's been ages and ages since we went in the car."

"He can sit next to me," said their mum, "so long as he doesn't wriggle."

It was midmorning by the time they set off, after a few false starts when the car spluttered and backfired. Eager noticed that Mr. Bell had a broad grin on his face as he steered the car onto the main road. "Are you going to drive?" asked his wife.

"To start with. The car can take over once we hit the motorway. Unless you want a go?"

"No, thank you. I think I've forgotten how."

For a long time they were the only car on the road, easily overtaking the delivery pods. "Careful," Mrs. Bell said instinctively each time her husband pulled out, but the oncoming pods swerved to let him pass.

They drove along by the learning center, which was swarming with families at the weekend, then skirted the technocrats' quarter. Gavin was surprised to see how far it stretched. It was the size of a small town and he had barely entered it on his visit to Marcia's house.

He imagined being Srin or Errol, looking in at the perfect replica houses, and kept away by robot patrols, walls and hot fences. No wonder the marauders were prepared to fight for change. Gavin checked his thoughts. He would probably never meet the boys again, and he had told himself not to think about them.

In any case, there were more pressing things to worry about—such as the BDC4s. Whatever his parents said, he was still suspicious of the robots. He knew that he wasn't always right, but he had a gut-wrenching feeling that there was something the matter with them. He glanced at Fleur to see if she shared his concern. She was gazing out of the window, a far-off expression on her face.

Beyond the technocrats' quarter they joined the motorway, three lanes of polished tarmac that stretched into the middle distance. There were no pods here. A few cars whizzed by but the traffic was so light that soon the cars were spaced out from each other.

"It's like the early days of motorway travel. Or so my grand-dad used to tell me," said Mrs. Bell. "Apparently the roads were empty and people would go for a drive on Sunday afternoon just out of interest."

"We're not so very different," said her husband, "with only two cans of petrol in the tank."

Gavin looked out of the window at the other cars on the road. Some were local vehicles like theirs, dating from the era when petrol was plentiful. He noticed that the cars which overtook them were more like pods, only a lot bigger and sleeker. They glided by, effortlessly and noiselessly. Most of them had tinted windows so it was impossible to see the passengers. Technocrats, obviously.

"That's where our petrol came from," observed Mr. Bell. He had handed the driving over to the car itself and was free to take a good look out of the window. They all followed his gaze, except Charlotte, who was asleep, and Fleur, lost in her otherworld.

Set back from the road was a tower with several outlying warehouses. A platoon of sightless robot miners was marching toward a row of hillocks behind the buildings.

"Decades of twentieth-century plastic," continued Mr. Bell, pointing toward the mounds. "Carrier bags, toys, bowls, pens, computers, light fittings, shoes, jewelry, toothpaste tubes, nappies . . . All waiting to be dug up and turned back into oil."

A question had always bothered Gavin. "Why is the recycled oil such bad quality? You'd think the technocrats could make better petrol by now."

"You're right," said his dad, "but for some reason it's proved hard to do. Of course, there's not much money spent on it. More money goes into inventing new robot technology and other sorts of fuel . . ."

"For the technocrats to use," said Gavin.

"It'll come to us eventually. By the time you're grown up I'm sure we'll have plenty of cheap clean fuel."

Eager had been wondering what it would be like to be a robot miner, burrowing into landfills. You would soon wear out, he imagined. "What happens to waste now?" he asked. The image of the dead robot came involuntarily to his mind.

"Space," replied Mrs. Bell. "We send it into outer space, way beyond the earth's orbit."

Everyone fell silent at the thought of myriad household objects spinning noiselessly in the void. The landfills disappeared from view.

"I don't suppose you two remember the songs we used to sing when you were little?" Mrs. Bell reminisced a while later.

"I do," Fleur said unexpectedly. "Doe, a deer . . ."

"Oh, no!" groaned Gavin. Then, whether it was the tug of memory or the pleasure of opening his lungs, he found himself joining in.

Eager listened politely. He was designed to reproduce human speech, and this singing was surely a musical form of speaking. Yet from the look on the Bells' faces, it was more enjoyable. He wondered what it would be like to ascend and descend in pitch, like nimbly climbing a ladder. He remembered the singing in the hotel and how the robots had danced to it. The memory was too painful. . . . But his curiosity proved stronger. He opened his mouth and released an experimental "Lah."

Mr. and Mrs. Bell nodded at him encouragingly as they started from the beginning again. He remembered the words from the first time. "Doe, a deer . . ." "Me, a name I call myself . . ." It was all true, but what did it mean? The Bells didn't seem to care. Like them, Eager gave himself up to the flow of sound.

"Did you enjoy that?" said Mrs. Bell.

"I think so."

The family burst out laughing. "We should try you with opera next," said Mr. Bell. "That'll give your voicebox an airing."

"I've never known a robot to enjoy music before," said his wife.

Eager made no comment.

CHAPTER 21

The car turned off the motorway onto a narrow undulating road. Mrs. Bell decided that she would drive after all. The countryside unfolded before them as she took the bends cautiously, yet expertly. There were fields now and hedges, and random sightings of spring flowers. Rabbits were everywhere and Gavin thought he saw a fox, which turned out to be a fallen branch. Meanwhile the gray clouds scudded across the sky, revealing patches of clear blue.

"Lovely day for a walk," said Mr. Bell. A message flashed on the screen on the dashboard: "Outward journey: fuel low." "Looks like we need to stop in any case."

"Who wants lunch before we walk?" asked Mrs. Bell, anticipating her children's approval. They pulled in at a farm that promised "good home cooking" and settled down at a vast wooden table in the kitchen. Grumps, released unscathed from the boot, sat Charlotte on his knee and prepared to feed her.

A robot served them but the farmer was at pains to stress

that she did all the cooking herself. "I enjoy it and I fancy it isn't the same when a machine does it. How do they know about that *je ne sais quoi* that makes food interesting, that's what I ask myself."

Through the brightly curtained window they saw four or five robot farmhands straggling across the yard. "Of course," continued the farmer, "it's wonderful to have them do the menial work. But my husband and I, we like to get our hands dirty. Why be on a farm otherwise? You might as well be in an office, I say. You're from the city, I suppose?" she said doubtfully.

"Professional quarter," replied Mrs. Bell, cutting herself a slice of quiche.

The woman nodded. "I could see you weren't technocrats by the car. If you'll pardon my saying so."

"It is a bit of a relic," agreed Mr. Bell.

"I thought you said it was 'vintage'?" said Gavin.

His parents laughed. "Wishful thinking," said his dad.

"You want a nice walk," interrupted the woman, "you should go through the woods here. You ask my husband; you'll see him working round the back as you pass."

Fleur's instinct as they entered the woods was to run. The path sloped downward enticingly and she let herself gather speed. She sensed that Gavin was behind her and for a moment they raced each other until the path petered out and trees blocked their way. They stopped beneath a silver birch to catch their breath. "Come on," said Fleur, and she was off again, running helter-skelter among the trees. Gavin at last caught up with her. "Stop a minute," he panted.

For the first time they were aware of their surroundings. They were under a broad lichen-covered tree, pale sunlight tilting at them through the branches. Tall smooth-barked beeches, standing to attention like friendly sentries, seemed to be waiting for them to speak. A bird sang piercingly.

"What are we going to do now?" said Gavin.

His sister stared at him. "What do you mean? There's nothing wrong. You're the only one who thinks there is."

Gavin was taken aback. He had imagined his sister to be as worried as he was. "What about Marcia? And Eager . . ."

"Eager!" Fleur spoke so scornfully that Gavin felt anger rising.

"You've changed your tune! Just because our plan didn't work. I know something's going on. You should have seen that Tibetan man's face yesterday when Dad mentioned Professor Ogden. And the way he looked at Eager—"

"You're not fighting, are you?" Mr. Bell had entered the clearing. He came over and put an arm around each of them, affectionately. "Only you both look cross."

"No," said Fleur. She glanced at Gavin but he had moved away and was kicking at a branch on the ground. Her brother had spoken so forcefully that she decided to test the situation one more time. "Dad, my gobepal from Nigeria called this morning. He said the BDC4s there held someone hostage, so

LifeCorp took all the robots back to the factory. Sarupa says LifeCorp did the same in Bombay."

Gavin had stopped kicking the branch. Fleur could almost feel his eyes boring into her but she was careful not to look round. He must not think that she agreed with him. She was just curious to know what her dad would say.

"Faults can happen," began Mr. Bell cautiously. "It doesn't mean all BDC4s are defective . . . a handful of robots from the same factory is not significant."

"That's what I thought," said Fleur, still avoiding Gavin's eye.

"Yoohoo!" Mrs. Bell, who was carrying the baby, and the two robots had caught up with them. "Charlotte insisted on walking but that means stopping every few seconds to poke in the mud!' laughed Mrs. Bell. "Here, you take her, Grumps. Which way now?"

"Bear right," said her jinn, which had recorded the farmer's instructions.

They set off together and began talking of other things. Gavin found himself walking with Eager, who was becoming increasingly excited. "It's all real," he kept repeating. His sharp eyes were sensitive to the slightest flurry and he ran from tree to tree, peering up into the branches to see what had caused the disturbance. At other times his eyes were pinned to the ground, following the scuttling of beetles and wood lice.

Gavin mulled over Fleur's news. If only he could agree with his dad that it meant nothing. He would have liked to tell Eager about the various incidents but decided that it would be unkind to involve him anymore.

"The trees are speaking to me," the robot announced.

Gavin was startled. "Are you sure?"

Eager nodded. "I feel waves coming at me. It's like when I sense the frequencies of other robots."

They were walking parallel to the rest of the party and could hear Fleur's laughter through the trees and Grumps' voice saying gravely, "That is a squirrel, Charlotte, not a pussy-cat."

"Am I alive?" asked Eager.

Gavin hesitated, not wanting to hurt the robot's feelings. "You're sort of alive because you can see and think and talk and move," he began. "But if you mean alive like the trees and the beetles and us, then no, you're not. You see, we're organisms and we can reproduce ourselves, and you're a machine."

"Squirrel, Charlotte," they heard Grumps say. "Not doggie."

Eager had gone quiet and stopped his inquisitive hurrying from tree to tree. The birdsong in the woods rose suddenly to a clamor.

"I once asked someone very clever on the gobey about this," continued Gavin. "He said it's like making a robot with a digestive system . . ."

"That would be useful. I was at a loss what to do while you were eating lunch."

"Yes, well . . . The food could go in and come out at the other end and even be broken down in the middle, but you still couldn't really eat pizza. Being alive is the same, apparently. There's some sort of process that makes it real that you don't have. Anyway," Gavin added encouragingly, "what's so wonderful about being like us?"

Eager gazed up at the sky. "I feel I am alive."

Gavin took a deep breath. He knew that the trees and the birds and the wood lice were all drawing on that same air for life. It was a connection that Eager would never have. Yet when he looked at Eager and saw the vibrant expression on his upturned face and the curiosity in his eyes he could not argue with him.

"Then you must be," he said.

Sounds of laughter and chatter were closer now as the others arrived, sidling and stooping through the branches. "This way," said Mrs. Bell. "We're nearly at the road. The farmer said if we turn left we'll soon be back at the farm."

The trees thinned and they could see a single-track road ahead of them. A lorry was parked a little way off. It wasn't a farm vehicle and its gray anonymity marked it out as an odd feature in the landscape. Gavin quickened his step, curious to find out what the lorry was doing.

He and Eager were the first out of the woods. They stepped into the lane and started walking toward the vehicle. Instantly, the engine started up, smooth and splutter-free. Gavin was too far away to see who was behind the wheel but an instinct stirred in him and he cried out to Eager, "Get back in the woods!"

Eager hesitated, wondering what the danger was. Then he heard the roar of the engine as the lorry accelerated toward him and he bounded into the trees. Mr. and Mrs. Bell and Fleur appeared and saw Gavin, waving his arms at them and shouting *"Stop!"* They stepped back onto the verge in confusion.

The lorry gathered speed. At that moment Grumps emerged from the woods further up, carrying Charlotte, and started to cross the road. There was an agonized scream from Mrs. Bell, the first to realize what was happening. Grumps turned at the sound to see the lorry bearing down on him; he spun round on his wheels as if to retreat, but it was too late. In a split second he had thrown Charlotte over his shoulder toward the trees. As she sailed through the air in a perfect arc Mrs. Bell rushed to catch her, but two strong rubbery arms got there first.

There was a terrible crash of metal hitting metal and the lorry thundered by. It rumbled in the distance; then all was sickeningly quiet. Sobbing with relief, Mrs. Bell ran to Eager and clutched Charlotte to her chest. The baby wriggled to escape, to signal that she wanted to play the flying game again. Fleur, Gavin and Mr. Bell gathered round and they hugged each other. They were in no rush to look at the scene behind them. Just for now they clung to the irrational but all too human hope that Grumps might somehow be put back together again.

At last Mr. Bell pulled away and walked slowly to the road. The children followed.

Scattered far and wide across the tarmac were heaps of mangled metal and twisted circuitry. A buckled wheel rolled drunkenly toward the verge. For a moment no one spoke. "I've got a shovel in the car," said Mr. Bell hoarsely.

"I'll help you, Dad," said Gavin.

"So will I," said Fleur. But when, further down the road, they spotted Grumps' motionless head, she burst into tears and ran to Mrs. Bell.

Gavin and his father walked the short distance to the farm and drove back in the car. They began to scoop up Grumps' remains, placing them in a blanket that had been on the backseat.

All this time Eager was standing at the side of the road, his system in turmoil. Life as he knew it had come to an end. How much worse it must be for the family. He went up to Mr. Bell. "Leave it to me," he said.

Mr. Bell shook his head. "With your hearing it's better you listen out for traffic." Fleur, her face puffy, came back to help and Eager went to stand in the middle of the road as they worked silently around him. The light was failing. He could hear the wind gathering in the trees and rooks shrieking.

They put the blanket in the boot and Mr. Bell slammed the door shut. Mrs. Bell insisted on squeezing into the back to be with the children so Eager had a front seat to himself. But he felt no pleasure in it as they drove, shocked and speechless, back to the suburb.

CHAPTER 22

That evening the older Bells carried on with their lives numbly, as if the lorry that had crushed Grumps had flattened them too. They spoke politely to each other and tiptoed around, anxious not to disturb the fragile fabric of their world. Charlotte was bad-tempered, refused to eat and whined all the time. Everyone agreed she must be teething. They all knew that really she was missing Grumps.

The next day Eager made a special effort and cooked pancakes for breakfast. Grumps had shown him how and though they were a little thick he was pleased with the results. He laid them on the table with a flourish. "Pancakes," he said, a note of pride in his voice.

An image flashed before the family of Grumps presenting them with a tureen of tomato soup. They couldn't help staring gloomily at Eager's offering. Gavin's eyes pricked with tears. Fleur dropped her fork, noisily.

"I was so horrible to him. I called . . . him . . . names," she choked. "Sometimes I wouldn't even . . . talk . . . to him . . . was ashamed."

"Come here," said her dad, holding out his arms to her. She sat on his knee, and for a moment sobbed uncontrollably.

Mr. Bell smoothed her hair. "Remember what I said? He was nothing more than a machine."

Fleur shook her head. "That's not what it feels like," she whispered.

"He was programmed to make us happy," persisted her father. "So if we smiled he would smile too. Other than that he didn't understand much about our moods. He wouldn't have known you were being rude."

"Your dad's right," said Mrs. Bell, kneeling beside them and putting her arm around Fleur.

"That's not what you said. You always wanted us to treat Grumps politely, like a person," said Fleur accusingly.

"I know I did. I didn't want us to take him for granted. I just wanted us to be grateful. Perhaps I overdid it."

Fleur began to cry again. "Grumps taught me to ride a bike—he used to hold on to it, do you remember? And he picked me up whenever I fell over and said 'No need for hospital,' which always made me cross. And only the other day he made my favorite pudding . . . I never asked him, he just did it!"

Gavin, flooded by his own memories, could not bear it anymore. He slid down from his chair and joined them. His dad put a hand on his shoulder and gave it a squeeze, while his mum hugged him with her free arm. He realized that she was crying too.

"We humans are a stupid lot," she sniffed, "making a fuss about a machine. There must be something about the way we're made. . . ."

"Even I miss him," said Mr. Bell, "after all I've said. Besides, it was a terrible accident. We didn't expect to lose him that way."

Fleur looked up, concern on her face. "Who's going to tell the kettle? Not me."

She was so indignant when the others began to laugh that they laughed even more. Fleur tried to get cross but found herself giggling and even Charlotte began to chuckle. Then Fleur started to hiccup, which set everyone off again.

Mrs. Bell wiped her eyes and stood up. "We may joke about it," she said, "but I'm going to visit the kettle. I think it would have been Grumps' last wish."

# # # # #

"We've got to talk," said Gavin.

Fleur put her finger to her lips. She led him out of the house and down to the wild patch at the bottom of the garden. "I don't want anyone or anything to overhear," she said in a low voice.

Gavin opened his eyes wide. "You mean . . . you think we can't trust our own house?"

"I think we can't take chances. I know what you're going to say," she went on. "The lorry in the woods, you think it was after Eager, don't you?" Her eyes were shining. "Did you see who was in it?"

"Not properly, but I'm sure it was robots. I think they meant to jump out and grab Eager."

Fleur sat down on the stone bench in the corner. "So who sent them?"

"I think it was LifeCorp." Gavin waited for his sister to protest; instead she bit her lip and looked askance at him.

"I was afraid you were going to say that," she muttered.

"It has to be!" he cried. "I bet it was the man we met at the hotel, Mr. Lobsang. He's one of LifeCorp's top robot designers. I told you—he looked at Eager with his tongue hanging out. These technocrats are just like the marauders, they want to get their hands on the latest technology. They're scared they might not be the first in the race—"

"Hang on," said Fleur. "I agree that LifeCorp probably wants to know what other scientists are doing. Perhaps this man thinks Eager is a rival product. But that doesn't mean he would kidnap Eager."

"Well, who else would?" Gavin wished his sister would stop trying to sound like a grown-up. She was so busy asking questions and weighing evidence that she couldn't see what was staring her in the face.

"And who else could, more to the point?" he said. "LifeCorp has hundreds of satellites in the sky. They know our address because Dad's working for them. It would be easy to spy on us. I bet they tracked us all the way to the woods and sent the lorry to meet us. But instead of getting Eager, they hit Grumps." He felt a wave of sadness at the memory.

After a moment he said bitterly, "I know one more thing—the robots wouldn't have done it on their own. It's against their laws. 'A robot must not harm another robot, unless instructed to by a human being.' "

Fleur let this sink in. "I still don't see why LifeCorp should be so interested in Eager."

"Because he's like the BDC4s, only different. Remember our conversation the other night? LifeCorp have spent years designing the BDCs, then along comes another robot that's just as clever as they are."

"But Mr. Lobsang only looked at Eager. How can he know anything about him?"

Gavin reflected. "I think he must know something about Professor Ogden's work. Listen, I think they might try again to get hold of Eager. That's what I wanted to talk to you about. We mustn't let him out of our sight from now on."

"Well, that won't be difficult," said Fleur, "since he's grounded." Her attention wandered to a speck of yellow beside the hedge. She pulled back the grass to find tiny primroses. Eventually she looked up at her brother. "Gavin, I'll help you with this. But I don't agree with you that the BDC4s are dangerous. They're just machines like all the other robots and sometimes machines can do funny things, that's all."

He frowned. "I can't help thinking there's a connection. Mr. Lobsang sees Eager as a rival to the BDC4s, and the BDC4s are behaving suspiciously."

She stood up. "I'm going back."

Gavin let her go past. He sighed, then followed her to the house. At the door she swung round. "Do you think we should tell him?" she said. "That LifeCorp is after him?"

Gavin thought of how dejected Eager had been since Grumps' accident. He did not want to add to his unhappiness. "No," he said.

■　■　■　■　■

Eager found the philosopher as usual, sitting on the bank under the tree and apparently wearing the same sheet.

"Hello," said Eager, which he had decided was the most neutral greeting he could give. It seemed to work, because the philosopher merely nodded and waited for him to continue.

"My friend Grumps has been run over," Eager began. "I think it was my fault, the lorry was chasing me, I'm sure of it. . . . I feel worse than when I put Charlotte in the washing machine."

He noticed that the philosopher was frowning.

"But this isn't what I want to ask about. Am I alive?"

The man clasped his hands together. "If you are here before me asking that question, how can you not be alive?"

Eager nearly retorted that the philosopher was there and he

was not alive, but he had a feeling that might get him into deep water.

"I forgot, you don't really understand—I'm a machine, not a living creature. But I've been thinking, there must be something more to it, being alive, than just being here and talking. You see, Grumps was a robot too and he 'died' when you unplugged his energy supply and then came to life again when you plugged him in. Only now he's really dead because he was destroyed—"

"Wait a minute," interrupted the philosopher. Eager noticed that there were beads of sweat on his forehead, although the sun was a long way from its highest point. "Aren't you the one who asked me about death the other day?"

"That's right," said Eager, delighted to be remembered.

"Go on," said the philosopher, sounding a trifle wary.

"Well, obviously there is something more to being alive. I can be turned on and off like Grumps, although I really don't like the idea and I certainly shan't volunteer for it ever to happen."

"Are you aware?"

"Aware of what?" said Eager.

"Aware that you exist?"

"Of course I am."

The philosopher raised an eyebrow. "It is thought that animals are not aware that they exist. At least, they cannot reflect on their actions. Can you?"

"You know I can!" exclaimed Eager. "I can think about my actions and choose how to behave."

The philosopher closed his eyes and pressed the tips of his fingers together. "Would you agree," he continued, opening his eyes, "that we are talking about free will?"

"Free Will?" said Eager. "Why, who locked him up? Is he a friend of yours?"

"I'm talking about choices," said the philosopher testily, and forgetting to speak in questions. "Whether we are really free to act or whether some greater power is controlling our actions."

"Grumps was controlled by a computer program. But I'm not and I'm sure humans aren't either," retorted Eager.

"I don't know about computer whatevers. What if the greater power created us and made us to believe that we are free to act?"

Eager considered this proposition. "Professor Ogden created me. But I don't believe he can be deciding how I behave. If he is," Eager reflected, "he's making some very funny decisions. I can't think why he wanted me to burn the toast this morning."

The philosopher was looking distinctly annoyed.

"The toaster's very old, you see, and Grumps was the only one who could work it properly," Eager said helpfully.

"How can I philosophize with you," stormed the philosopher, "when you insist on going off on tangents and superfluities?"

"I haven't gone off on anything!" protested Eager. "I'm still here."

The philosopher leant back against the tree and mopped his brow with a corner of the sheet. "I regret that I am not the right teacher for you," he sighed. "I will arrange for another philosopher to take over. Excuse me." He vanished.

Eager sat on the bank and waited for several minutes but no one appeared. For some reason it was taking the new teacher a long time to arrive. He would have to return another day.

CHAPTER 23

The following morning Mr. Bell accompanied Fleur and Gavin to the learning center on his way to work. The novelty of the situation was a poignant reminder that things had changed. Although the weather was warm and cloudless, the children trudged along with somber faces.

"Dad," said Fleur, "will we be getting a new robot soon?"

"We don't need a new robot," said Gavin, "we've got Eager. Have you spoken to Professor Ogden, Dad? I bet he knows what's going on."

" 'Fraid not. The gobey keeps saying he's inaccessible."

"You can't take us to the center every day," said Fleur.

Mr. Bell stroked his jaw. "I know, you're embarrassed to be seen with your old dad. Well, I happened to mention to one of the technocrats at the factory that we'd lost Grumps. You'll never believe what he said. He's offered us a BDC4."

He looked nervous, as if he expected a hostile response. "I know you two aren't fond of the BDC4s . . ."

"Anything's better than nothing," said Fleur. "But we don't want a groveling one like Boadicea."

"I bet they're all groveling," said Gavin.

"I haven't got time to discuss this now," said their father hastily. They had reached the gates to the learning center. "My hoverbus is due any second. You go on in. We'll talk— What on earth?"

The cause of his astonishment was a figure running along the pavement toward them. The children turned and saw Marcia, her coat flapping to reveal the orange-blue dress glowing violently. She reached them and doubled over, panting to get her breath back.

"What's wrong?" said Fleur.

Marcia said gasping, "Mum and Dad . . . Boadicea's kidnapped them. And BJ. She's trapped them in the house—"

"Can you kidnap someone in their own home?" said Fleur pedantically.

Marcia gave her a stricken look. "Sorry," said Fleur.

"What do you mean, trapped?" said Mr. Bell. "Have you called the police?"

Marcia nodded. "They've surrounded our quarter. Boadicea isn't the only one, you see. All the BDC4s . . . they've taken over the other houses. But the police can't do anything so long as they're holding people hostage. . . ." She began to sob. Fleur put an arm around her.

"Where are you off to?" said Mr. Bell.

215

"LifeCorp headquarters. Dad told me to run, I was outside when Boadicea closed the walls on them . . ."

Fleur shuddered, remembering her own experience.

". . . and he shouted after me to find some man at headquarters."

"Not Mr. Lobsang?" said Gavin.

Startled, Marcia said, "How do you know?"

"He helped design the BDC4s," said Mr. Bell. "I'm building a factory for him."

Behind the tears, Marcia's face lit up. "Will you take me to him?"

Mr. Bell looked regretful. "Marcia, I'm sorry about what's happened. But Mr. Lobsang is bound to have been told already. I'm sure he's doing all he can to control the BDC4s. One more person going to him won't change the situation. There's no need for you to get involved."

Fleur had seen before the stubborn look that now spread over Marcia's face. "He and my dad used to work together," said the technobrat. "If he knows Dad's in trouble he might try harder to . . ." She started to sob again.

"All right," sighed Mr. Bell. "You may as well come with me to the factory. We can't leave you in the street, in any case. If Mr. Lobsang isn't there, we'll send him a message."

"Can't we come too?" said Fleur. Her dad gave her a reproving look.

"We haven't seen the new factory yet," added Gavin, "and

with all that's happening, how are we going to concentrate on our work?"

Mr. Bell shrugged helplessly. "I'm sure you're right. Come on, let's catch that hoverbus."

▪ ▪ ▪ ▪ ▪

"It's such a lovely day. Why don't you take Charlotte for a walk in the garden?"

Eager looked round at Mrs. Bell. "Me?" he said. "Are you sure?"

Mrs. Bell was fastening Charlotte's coat. "Just for a few minutes while I get ready for work. Then I'm taking her with me to the day care center." She stood up. "I'll be upstairs in the office so I can keep an eye on you both from the window in case anything happens."

Eager pondered the significance of Mrs. Bell's words. "I shan't do anything bad, if that's what you mean," he said.

Mrs. Bell smiled ruefully. "Eager, I'm sure you wouldn't do anything wrong deliberately but I can't take any chances. Look how Grumps behaved when his timer wore out! For all I know, some of what the children say about the BDC4s might well be true. If advanced robots like that can behave strangely, well . . . perhaps you can too." She sighed. "I really don't know what to think anymore, where robots are concerned."

"I understand," said Eager.

217

He carried Charlotte through the front door and set her down on the path. Despite the warm sun there was a chill in the air. Charlotte was so bundled up in her coat that she looked like a balloon. Eager was convinced that if she toppled over she would roll down the garden path. He watched her carefully as she tottered two or three steps. She stopped and pointed at a gray cat on the lawn. Eager followed her gaze and the cat stared back at him with saucer eyes.

A second later the cat whisked its head round as if it sensed something behind it. Eager heard a faint buzz and saw the distant speck of a pod, curving toward them in the sky. The cat arched its back and leapt over the wall. Eager quickly picked up Charlotte. It was too late to get back to the house. He hurried to the lime tree and shrank down until they were out of sight from the road.

"Shhh," he murmured, and bobbed his head to encourage her to pull at his nose.

Eager had thought a lot about the events in the woods. Over and over again his mind replayed the image of the lorry accelerating toward him. The robots at the wheel had been seeking him, he was certain of it. And now, with the unexpected arrival of the pod, perhaps they had come to try again. As best he could he peered into the road. The pod had come down outside the house; he could just see the top of it over the Bells' low wall.

He turned back to Charlotte, willing her to be quiet. He waited, counting the minutes before someone would appear on the path beside the tree, but no one did. He stole another look and saw the robot from next door standing beside the pod. Charlotte began to whine crossly so he let her pull his nose again. When next he peeped out the robot was walking back to the house with a parcel in its hand and the pod was rising into the air.

"Silly me," he said to Charlotte, who chuckled at him. But perhaps it was not so foolish to be alarmed. He could hardly treat every delivery pod that came to the avenue as a threat. Yet if he stayed with them the Bells might be in danger. He bounced Charlotte on his knee, feeling how fond he was of her. There was only one thing to do.

※ ※ ※ ※ ※

The hoverbus carrying Mr. Bell and the children flew over the professional quarter to the outskirts of the city. The sky grew busy with flying pods.

Gavin was looking at the city with fresh eyes since his encounter with the marauders. It was not the hopeless place he had once imagined it to be. Remembering Errol's passionate words, he half expected to see signs of unrest, but all seemed orderly enough. He spotted a group of robots scrubbing a fountain, and several others weeding the grass verges. Bicycles and pedestrians moved rhythmically along the streets.

They passed rows of converted office blocks, and Gavin could not suppress a thought that one of the shuttered apartments might be home to Errol or Srin. What were they doing now? he wondered. Trawling, perhaps. He tried to imagine what would happen if the city people succeeded in creating a world without boundaries, and turned to dreaming of possible futures for himself. . . .

Fleur watched her fellow passengers as they read a lexiscreen or stared pensively through the window. It amazed her that in the midst of her own drama other people should be carrying on their normal life. She glanced at Marcia, who sat white-faced beside her. Her father looked round and smiled reassuringly. "Next stop," he said.

As they left the city the buildings thinned out. A wide open space greeted them when they stepped down from the hoverbus. Mr. Bell turned to the right along a newly laid road flanked by a high wall. From the telltale ripples of air above it, the wall was protected by a heat barrier. Gavin recalled the hot fence at the technocrats' quarter. How stupid of him not to have spotted that it was turned off.

"Do you always take the bus?" Marcia asked Mr. Bell, as they strode along. "If my dad has an important meeting somewhere, LifeCorp sends a flying pod for him."

"They did offer to fetch me every day," said Mr. Bell, "but I like a walk. And it isn't far."

Now that Marcia sounded more like herself, Fleur was encouraged to voice the question she was dying to ask. "Marcie, what exactly did Boadicea do?"

"It started days ago," said Marcia, her eyes bright with the recollection. "She was behaving as if she owned everything. Instead of 'the' house she began to say 'my' house. She would put on music that she liked and went off with other robots without telling us. She stopped helping me with my work and she wouldn't chat anymore. When I told her off she didn't seem to be listening.

"Then this morning after breakfast she took over the controls of the whole house. Everything happened at once—the walls moved, the doors locked . . . she must have set things up earlier. Luckily I'd just gone into the garden to pick daffodils—I wanted to paint them today—and so I escaped. She looked furious when she realized. I stood outside the kitchen; everyone was calling to me but I couldn't hear. Mum started shooing me, I knew she wanted me to run off but Dad seemed to have a message . . . Then he came through on my jinn and managed to tell me about Mr. Lobsang. The jinn went dead; Boadicea must have turned off the gobey somehow. I ran and ran to the entrance and a group of BDC4s—they were marching like soldiers—nearly caught up with me. They must have been going to take over the gate and I got through just in time."

Fleur squeezed Marcia's arm. "My gobepal in Nigeria said that BDC4s imprisoned someone at the oil fields. But LifeCorp switched off their power and everything was all right."

Marcia said nothing. She kept her eyes ahead, her face expressionless, so that it was impossible to tell what she was thinking.

"Here we are." Mr. Bell stopped outside a titanium gate. He stood square-on for its optical sensors to scan his eyes. A panel in the gate slid open. "Wait here while I get clearance for you," he said.

Moments later the panel opened again and the children entered. Ahead of them, beyond a paved forecourt, was a single-story building, its sides curling in and out to form a vast figure of eight. The walls were white and porcelain-smooth. There were no windows or doors. Enormous glass panes made up the roof, each one gently curved like a wave on a lake. To the side of the building was a domed glass structure.

"It's beautiful, Dad," breathed Fleur. "I'm so proud of you."

Mr. Bell raised an eyebrow. "Glad you approve."

"Euphoric," said Gavin. "So the roof acts as a window?"

"That's right. And there are doors, believe it or not! You need to get up close to see them. They must be tightly sealed to avoid contamination, so we made that a feature of the design."

"You built it so quickly," said Fleur.

"Yes," said her dad, "thanks to a huge workforce of robots."

"What's that igloolike building?" said Gavin.

"Good morning, Mr. Bell." A man in gray overalls had come up to them.

"Morning. I've had to bring my children today, and this is a friend of ours. Her parents are caught up in some trouble at the technocrats' quarter."

The man looked uncomfortable as he faced Marcia. "Shocking news," he said gruffly. "We're all on security alert because of it. Rum lot, these BDC4s. But don't you worry, it's just a matter of shutting down their power. LifeCorp's safety record is second to none, as I'm sure you know." He turned to Mr. Bell. "Our BDC4s have gone back to headquarters for tests. There won't be much work done today."

"No," agreed Mr. Bell. "We'd come to rely on them a lot, hadn't we?"

"The site manager is waiting for you in the office, to talk things over."

"Is Mr. Lobsang here?" said Marcia.

The man was taken aback, either by the question or the agitation in her voice. "Well, he's at headquarters, I believe."

"Why don't you wait for me in the recreation room?" said Mr. Bell to the children, indicating a low mobile building beside the gate. "I'll try not to be long; then we can see about contacting Mr. Lobsang. If there's any news I'll come to find you at once."

He and the man crossed the forecourt and Gavin and Fleur set off toward the low building. "Aren't you coming?" said Gavin, when Marcia did not move.

"If you think I'm going to hang around at a time like this . . ."

"What else can we do," said Fleur, "except wait?"

"You don't see, do you?" said Marcia.

"See what?"

Marcia screwed up her face in annoyance. "Everyone keeps saying that it's just a question of shutting down the robots.

223

Well, why haven't they? I mean, how long does it take to close down a radio frequency?"

"You said yourself there are transmitters everywhere," said Gavin. "There must be several within range. Perhaps it takes longer than you think."

"But they can do it," Fleur burst out. "I told you what Chike said."

Marcia said fiercely, "Didn't you see that man just now? He couldn't look me in the eye when he was talking about the robots. There's something going on and I'm not waiting round here like a moonrock." She set off at a run toward the new building and stopped in front of the glass igloo. Gavin and Fleur shrugged at each other and followed.

"Thought so," she panted. "It's a lift to the underground network. It must go to headquarters." The lift doors opened and Marcia grinned for the first time. "That's lucky. No one's set the security code."

A nanosecond later, it seemed to Gavin, they were at the bottom of a shaft. Lights came on as they stepped out of the lift. "It's a tunnel!" he cried.

"What did I tell you?" said Marcia.

In fact, there were three tunnels, tapering away into blackness. At the entrance to each was a small open-roofed train. "How do you know where they go?" said Fleur.

Marcia called out, "LifeCorp headquarters," and the train nearest to her rose. She climbed into a carriage. "Well?"

"I think we should stay," said Fleur solemnly. "There's

nothing we can do at the headquarters. And Dad will be worried to death if we all disappear."

"Marcia . . . ," said Gavin. He stopped. He had an instinct to warn her about Mr. Lobsang, but he was not sure how to explain it. "Nothing. Just . . . be careful."

"Go," Marcia commanded. She shot forward in the hovertrain without a backward glance.

It suddenly felt cold in the shaft. Gavin and Fleur climbed back into the lift, which, sensing their weight, began its ascent. Back at ground level they heard a shout. Their father, the man in gray overalls and four or five others ran toward them.

"Where's Marcia?" cried Mr. Bell.

"She's gone to LifeCorp's headquarters," said Fleur. Her dad looked less angry than she had expected, though his face was ashen.

"Probably the best place for her," said the man in overalls. "The technocrats can reassure her and keep her informed of what's happening."

"What's going on, Dad?" said Gavin, realizing that his father's paleness had nothing to do with Marcia.

Mr. Bell took a deep breath. "It's your mum. She just called . . . there's a problem at the hotel."

"Not the BDC4s!" exclaimed Fleur.

"Yes, there's some difficulty shutting them down. Charlotte's in the day care center . . . I said I'd go there straightaway."

"We'll call a pod," said a woman wearing a yellow hard hat.

"Thank you."

"What about us?" said Fleur.

Her father put an arm around her. "You're coming too. We're going to keep together. Your mum said there's no danger, though it sounded like chaos at the hotel."

Gavin fell into step beside them. "Dad, we'd better call Eager and tell him what's going on."

It was a second or two before Mr. Bell replied. He looked gravely at his son. "I'm sorry, Gavin. Your mum called the house and . . . Eager's gone."

CHAPTER 24

Eager's main concern before he left was how to provide the family with food that evening. He knew that they would come back from work hungry. He confided in the oven.

"Cooking is a pleasure, never a chore!" it gushed.

"What if there's no time?" said Eager.

"Chicken pie, meat compartment, freezer," the oven said sharply.

"Thank you," said Eager.

"And peas. Top drawer, freezer."

Eager placed the pie in the oven and emptied the peas into a saucepan on top of the hob.

"Leave it to me," said the oven.

"Thank you," said Eager.

He made a final check of the kitchen, quickly turning away from the spot where Grumps used to recharge his batteries. So much had happened since that first night when the butler had shocked Eager by turning himself off. Eager walked down the hallway, pausing by the front door.

"House, tell the Bells that . . . I'm sorry to leave them. I'm going back to Professor Ogden. Say that I don't want to cause them any more trouble."

"I shall reproduce your message exactly," said the house.

Eager stepped into the garden. For the first time in his life, it was up to him to decide where he went and what he did. With a backward look at the lime tree, he turned into the avenue and hurried along to the nearest bus stop. A hoverbus soon came. As he climbed aboard, a message was scrolling across the screen: ". . . conductor for today is Dora. Patrons are advised that . . ."

"Code?" said the conductor, blocking Eager's way into the body of the bus.

"Which code?" said Eager.

"That is what I am asking you," said Dora. "You must tell me your code to prove that you are authorized to travel on this hoverbus."

Eager thought back to his last trip. Mr. Bell had taken care of everything then. "I was not asked for one before," he said.

"I do not know the circumstances. All unaccompanied robots must provide a code number."

Eager tilted his head. "Fifty-nine?" he said hopefully.

"Incorrect," said Dora.

"Is it a larger number?" said Eager, hoping to narrow the probability of guessing it.

"You are trying to pull a fast one," said Dora. "I am programmed to spot that. If you do not know the code number you must alight at the next stop."

"But that isn't where I'm going! I shall be lost."

"Then I shall direct you to the nearest terminus to await collection."

"Await collection?" said Eager hotly. "I am not a parcel!"

The conductor took a step closer to him and Eager understood that she was not going to give in. He tried a different tack. "Dora, I must go to the city. If not, humans may suffer. You cannot allow that to happen, can you?"

He sensed her uncertainty. "You must not let harm come to humans, must you, Dora? Therefore you should let me continue on my way."

The conductor's most ingrained programming took the upper hand. She stood aside. "Very well."

Eager clung to a pole in the center of the hoverbus and kept a careful lookout through the window. From the corner of his eye he could tell that people were staring at him. At last he spotted the park that he had seen on the previous journey. A little later the hoverbus swooped down to pick up a passenger and Eager climbed off.

He walked along narrow streets that he remembered from last time, though now he was making the journey in reverse and had to keep stopping and looking both ways to make sure that he was on the right path. He was surprised not to see Sphere, showing him the way once more.

Soon he was standing on the steps of Professor Ogden's house. It was midday and the street was quiet.

Even before he knocked he knew that there would be no response. The house was empty. Eager peered through one of the windowpanes and felt disappointed when Sphere did not float out. Perhaps he had been doing the right thing, so there was no need for the ball's help. But surely now he needed guidance.

A young woman was patiently helping a baby mount the steps to a neighboring house. Eager went over to her. He remembered to smile at the baby to show that he was friendly. Nonetheless the woman bent down and pulled the child close to her.

"Excuse me, I'm looking for Professor Ogden. Do you know him? Do you know where he's gone?" said Eager.

The woman smiled. "He's very friendly," she said, "always asking me what new thing my baby can do! I did hear noises— if he's gone I think they went in the night." She entered a card in the lock and opened the front door. "A car came," she called after Eager. "I wouldn't mistake that sound. We haven't had a car in this street for years."

Eager felt in great turmoil, as if his system had been turned upside down. He knew that most city people could not afford cars or petrol. So who could have come for the professor in the night? He rounded the corner into the next street, knowing that there was only one answer to his question.

The next moment his system *was* upside down and the rest of him with it, as the ground slipped from under him. He reached out to steady himself and found that he was caught in a mesh of thin steel. He clawed at it and his fingers slipped through the holes. The net jerked backward. He felt the mesh tighten. A new feeling overwhelmed him—it was fear, he realized, fear that the harsh wire would cut into his rubber. He curled into a ball and let himself be dragged along.

"A fine trawl," said a man's voice, close to his ear. Eager had heard that word before. The marauders had used it. Then he was tumbling down as if a hole in the earth had opened up. A hard surface met him. The net loosened and he flopped his limbs to the ground. At first there was darkness around him; then a light came on and he decided to close his eyes.

"It's Ogden's work, I'm sure of it." It was the man who had first spoken. Someone grunted. "So it could be a LifeCorp robot, after all," the man continued.

"Are you mad?" said a second man in a reedy voice. "Ogden would sooner die than build another robot for the corporation."

There was a pause.

"That's what he wants us to believe," said the first man.

"Whatever do you mean?"

"Remember what happened? The professor turns up and says he's quarreled with the technocrats and wants to build a lab in the city. Naturally, we welcome him. But what if the whole thing was a trick? He's still with the technocrats and all this time he's been spying on us."

A woman's voice spoke. "I'm sure our professor friend has

better things to do than spy on us. But suppose he *is* still working for LifeCorp? What if he's been building the new super-robot right under our noses? We're worried about the BDC4s but perhaps they're a smokescreen. Perhaps this robot here is the real danger to us."

"Preposterous!" said the thin-voiced man. "Just look at this. Call it a super-robot? Next to a BDC4 it's like a chicken to a peacock!"

Eager's head shot up in indignation and he quickly lowered it. No one seemed to have noticed.

"Well, I need some lunch," said the woman. "I haven't eaten all day. Have the boys brought food?"

"Not yet," said the first man. "All right, we'll examine this robot later. He hasn't moved. Let's hope we haven't damaged him."

Eager listened out for their retreating footsteps, then struggled once more with the steel net. Someone had fastened it at the end and though it hung loosely about him it was impossible to crawl out. He had the strength to rip apart many things but not this taut metal. He lay there in the darkness, running over in his mind the conversation he had just heard. They had been talking about Professor Ogden—*his* Professor Ogden—as if he were a bad, cunning person. Eager told himself that it could not be true.

He heard a scuttling noise and closed his eyes again.

"Let's have a look at you," said a slow voice. There was an exclamation. "It's the robot with the arms!"

Eager knew that voice. He opened his eyes. Srin was crouching beside him, illuminated by the thin beam of a laser.

"What's going on?" Light flooded the room. In a narrow doorway stood the woman. Eager managed to sit up and look at her. She had a lean face that seemed familiar to him. But her hair intrigued him most. He had never seen hair like it before. It appeared to grow in fine black ropes, held back from her face by a thick band.

"I know this robot," said Srin. "Saved us from the police."

Two men had followed the woman into the room. The taller one frowned. "What's this nonsense?" he said in the thin voice Eager had heard before.

"He helped us," repeated the boy. "He's not LifeCorp, he's different."

"He certainly is," said the woman, sounding gentler than before. "That's why we want to examine him."

Srin jumped up. "Don't do that! You might spoil him!"

"Just because you feel grateful," murmured the woman, "we can't stop our scientific investigation. Now, off you go."

The boy looked down at Eager with a sullen expression. "You wouldn't hurt us, would you?"

Eager shook his head energetically.

"See!" said Srin to the woman.

"We aren't interested in what he says!" she cried. "We want to know how he works. Now, go!"

Under her fierce gaze Srin sidled past the two men and out of the door.

"It seems to be functioning all right," said the woman, glancing at Eager. "Let's get the equipment ready."

She and the two men walked off. Once more Eager was plunged into gloom. At the professor's house, in the room under the eaves, darkness was comforting and familiar. Now it held terrors for him. He found himself remembering the robot lying still in the back of a van, and the sight of Grumps' scattered remains on the road.

A thin beam of light reappeared. Something was moving in the shadows. "Robot," whispered a voice, "it's Errol. I'm going to let you out. Keep still."

There was a tug at the net and he heard the sound of wire snapping. Errol cut and pulled at the mesh for several minutes, swearing under his breath. "Should be big enough," he said at last. The torch resting on the floor cast a shallow pool of light that was hard to see by. It took Errol a while to feel his way and ease the net over the robot's head. Eager crawled out. The boy stood up, pulling the robot with him.

"Hurry," he whispered. "They'll be back soon."

Outside the room was a corridor. Errol turned off the torch. Still holding Eager's arm, he led him through the darkness and up a narrow staircase. There was a delay while Errol seemed to be pushing against something; then they continued climbing. Eager found himself in daylight. Glancing back, he saw a door cut into the floor. He stared curiously at it.

Errol said, "In the old days it's where people used to drop

sacks of wheat and things into the cellar. Now it's a robot trap."
He grinned but Eager felt alarmed.

"How did they catch me?"

"They've been watching that professor's house for ages.
Soon as they saw you they called for the net."

"Why were they—"

A low whistle interrupted him. Srin came running round
the corner. "What you doing? Sunbathing?"

Errol pulled at Eager's arm. "Come on!"

"Where are you taking me?" he said.

The boy raised his eyebrows in mock surprise. "To see your
professor, where else?"

CHAPTER 25

The marauders led him so quickly through the streets that Eager barely had time to notice his surroundings, let alone ask questions. At last they reached a busy road, teeming with pods. "This is where we hitch a lift," Errol said, smiling.

Eager watched the pods as they whirred along. Some of them gathered speed and became airborne.

"Need a big one for three of us," said Srin. "Gotcha!" He and Errol had grabbed a pod and were straining backward to prevent it taking off. The other pods swerved to avoid it. "Quick!" shouted Errol as the pod began to slip away from them. Eager hesitated, then sprang onto the roof. He stretched out his arms and hoisted the boys to his side.

The pod wobbled precariously beneath their weight and slowly rose. It joined scores of flying pods traveling in the same direction. Eager looked down through the glass roof to see a bewildered robot worker staring back at him. Eager waved politely. Raising his voice above the wind, he said, "Who were those people?"

"That was Errol's mum," said Srin with relish. "She'll go bananas."

"That's not what he meant, wetbrain. They're city scientists," said Errol. "The cellar they put you in is just a front."

"It seemed more like a bottom to me," remarked Eager.

"I mean a disguise. So no one would guess there's a brilliant laboratory next door." He noticed that Eager was puzzled. "It's like we said the other day—it's illegal to be a scientist without permission. You need a license from the government."

"Why?" said Eager.

"Technology's supposed to be dangerous in the wrong hands," said Errol, adding scornfully, "Tell that to LifeCorp."

A dreadful feeling came over Eager. Could the "wrong hands" mean Professor Ogden? "What did the professor do?" he said. "Please tell me."

"Nothing's proved," said Errol, "but people have suspicions. He used to be a technocrat. Yep, he worked for LifeCorp. The story goes, he didn't like the research they were doing. Said it was dangerous. There's a big row and he leaves, buys a house in the city. The city scientists get excited, they think he's going to join 'em. But he says no, he's setting up his own laboratory. Now some people have started to say it was all a hoax. That really LifeCorp sent him to find out what the city scientists are doing."

"That's stupid, though," said Srin. "If he wanted to spy on 'em, he'd go ahead and join 'em, wouldn't he?"

"Haven't you heard of double bluff?"

Eager tilted his head. He needed all the thinking power he could get. "So that's when he began to build robots like me—when he came to the city?"

"Looks like it."

"The man back there thought I might be a LifeCorp robot."

"Well, are you?" said Srin.

Eager bowed his head. "I don't know." He thought back to his days in the professor's house. Nothing had happened that seemed to be anything other than what it was. But perhaps the professor had been playing a clever game with him too. He was busy contemplating this when Srin shouted, "Headquarters!"

Errol laughed at Eager's amazement. "Yep, LifeCorp's headquarters. That's where the professor's gone."

Ahead of them a glass-and-titanium building rose sheer from the ground, surrounded by a high metal wall. "Lie down!" said Errol as the squadron of pods flew over the barrier. "This is how we get inside," he said. "Hundreds of pods come here every day so no one watches 'em closely."

Landscaped grounds, dotted with bushes and flowering trees, stretched out below them. Eager sat up. From close to, the glass building looked like a huge ship carved out of ice. On the roof, where a ship's prow might have been, balanced a gigantic red-and-gray ball.

The pod swooped down to a side entrance, where its passengers jumped off. It joined the ranks of tens of other delivery pods hovering by the door. "This is where we leave you," said Errol.

"Thank you," said Eager. "How will you get out?"

"Wait for another ride," laughed Srin.

Errol lowered his voice. "You might as well go in at the front. Ask for Professor Ogden. I'd like to see their reaction, but we can't risk getting caught."

They said goodbye and ran off toward a clump of bushes. Eager waved farewell to the robot worker in the pod, and walked round to the front of the building. Far above him a pane of glass detached itself and glided downward.

"Sphere!" cried Eager. He sounded reproachful and wished he hadn't. "I thought you might have helped me earlier," he explained.

The ball hovered above him, its outline clear against the sky.

Images came into Eager's head, as in a dream: Sphere was guiding him from the professor's house, through the streets, all the way to LifeCorp's headquarters. Once there, he could not get over the wall. . . .

"I understand," he said. "Everything had to happen the way it did. If I hadn't been caught I wouldn't have met the boys again and I wouldn't have found out about the professor and I wouldn't have got here on a delivery pod." He tilted his head as a thought struck him. "But you could have told me where to go, what to do. I would have understood."

Sphere blazed with light.

"Perhaps," mused Eager, "I can only see a bit of the truth. Like looking through a doorway and seeing half a table. There's a bigger view I don't know about. Perhaps I had to meet the scientists and the marauders had to come here. . . ."

The rays shone so brightly that Eager took a step backward. And in that moment he learnt something else. He was about to face the hardest test of all.

* * * * *

Sphere floated ahead of the robot until they reached an immense titanium door that drew back with a subtle whoosh. Eager was surprised not to be stopped, but perhaps the door had recognized him as a robot and decided that he was staff. He and Sphere entered LifeCorp's headquarters.

Eager found himself standing directly beneath the roof of the building. The glass vault was so high that he had to bend backward to look at it. As he watched, Sphere flew up and up until it became a distant particle that merged with the glass. Eager waited for some time; when the ball did not reappear he walked on.

Beyond the cavernous entrance the building was divided into floors. Eager followed a corridor straight ahead of him. There was no one about, human or robot. He walked for some time until he reached a seating area opposite a row of lifts. A girl with dark hair looked round at his approach. "I've seen you before . . . ," she began, frowning. "I know! You came to my house with Gavin. What are you doing here?"

Before Eager could reply she said, "Of course, the Bells sent you to see that I was safe."

"No," said Eager without thinking. He realized his mistake when the girl, who he remembered was called Marcia, frowned at him again. He said quickly, "I came of my own accord," which pleased him because it was the truth, although it did not answer Marcia's question directly.

"Your own accord? You mean, you chose to come?" Marcia stared in amazement. "I've been looked after by robots all my life, and never, ever has a robot been concerned about me from choice."

Eager began to feel that the misunderstanding had gone too far. But he was silenced by the dramatic change in her expression. Unknown to him, it was the look that came over her when she stood before one of her favorite paintings in a gallery: a mixture of awe and gratitude.

"Are you sure no one sent you to find me?" she said at last.

"Quite sure," said Eager, delighted to be direct for once.

Marcia turned her head away from him for a moment. When she faced him again she was her usual self.

"I came to see Mr. Lobsang," she said crossly. "The technocrats say he isn't here. So I insisted on talking to the person in charge. They told me to wait. That was ages ago. People have been running all over the place and now they've gone upstairs and won't let me go with them."

A lift door opened and a man and a woman, both in gray overalls, came out. "There you are," said the woman to Marcia.

"What's that?" said the man.

Eager had heard this question so many times that his patience was wearing thin. "How rude—"

Marcia stood up and grabbed his arm. "Play dumb," she whispered. "This is my personal robot. I made him myself as part of a project. I'm very proud of him."

The technocrats laughed, though not unkindly. "So you should be. What's it built with?" asked the woman.

"A quantum transistor, neural networks and . . . er . . . holographic memory system," Marcia reeled off confidently. "It was a first attempt so naturally he's a bit clunky."

Clunky! Eager hung his head and drooped his arms in a bid to look as clunky as possible.

"The head of robotics is ready to see you now." The woman led them into the lift. She took them up to a spacious room with high windows, and left them. It was dusk outside and the lighting in the room was low. At the far end, beside a small table, stood a stocky figure with white hair. Marcia waited by the door, uncertainly. Eager saw the face he knew so well, and the world began to spin.

"EGR3," said a gentle voice, "it's all right." The man had stepped forward and was looking closely at him. Eager focused his gaze on Professor Ogden's eyes and recognized the same quality he had seen in the room under the eaves.

"That look in your eyes . . . ," he began.

"Is a kind one."

Memories of his early life flashed through Eager's brain. Every night the professor had been at his side, questioning, teaching, encouraging him. Now they were together again. Yet he knew that it was impossible to return to the simple days of the creator and his creation. Eager was changed from the robot that had left the laboratory, and though he looked the same, the man had changed too.

"If you're so kind," piped up an imperious voice, "why is one of your robots holding my family prisoner?"

Professor Ogden turned to Marcia and held out his hands in a gesture of regret. "It's been a long time since I had anything to do with these robots. I can assure you that things will be different from now on."

Eager tilted his head. He remembered telling the philosopher that Professor Ogden was good. But the professor had disappeared without a word and here he was, taking charge of the corporation that he claimed to have quarreled with. "Professor Ogden," said Eager, "I'm not sure I trust you."

The professor smiled. A little wistfully, however. "Good. Then I have achieved my aim of creating a robot that can truly think for itself."

"So that's who you are!" exclaimed Marcia. "I know all about you. You used to work for LifeCorp but you had to leave because you were a traitor."

"Well, well, well . . . ," murmured the professor. He indicated an arrangement of soft chairs in the corner. "Shall we sit down? I've nothing to offer you, I'm afraid, and everyone is rather busy at the moment. Ah, here is some cake. Most fortuitous . . ."

"What are you doing here?" Marcia asked, cutting a slice of fruitcake. "Are you really in charge?"

"I am indeed. I was summoned here by my former colleagues. Yes," he said, seeing the look on her face, "I was surprised too. The head technocrats came to my house yesterday evening. They wanted my help to avert a crisis. Apparently they've been watching my activities with interest over the years." He paused and stared at his feet for a moment. "Do you know the story of Icarus?"

Marcia shook her head, her mouth full of crumbs.

"He and his father were imprisoned by the King of Crete—most ungrateful of the king. Icarus' father was a very clever engineer, you see, but he knew too many secrets. They plotted to escape by building themselves wings made out of wax. It must have taken them a while but at last they set off and all was well. Icarus and his father were overjoyed at the success of their invention. They flew on, high above the sea. Then Icarus grew too bold. Without considering the consequences, he flew higher and higher toward the sun until the heat began to melt his wings and down he plunged, into the sea."

"He must have known his wings would melt," Marcia said scornfully.

"I'm sure he did. But at what point did he forget?" The professor smiled.

"It isn't true," said Marcia, "it's a Greek myth. Why are you telling me it?"

"I see it as a lesson to us all. Sometimes we have to fly close to the sun because part of being human is to reach for things beyond us. The secret is to know when to stop."

He rose and began to pace up and down. Eager watched him anxiously, hoping he would become the cheerful professor he remembered. Was this how it felt to be a parent, he wondered, longing to spare your child from unhappiness?

The professor spoke again. "There used to be a group of us—myself, Mr. Lobsang and others—dedicated engineers who discovered the secret of artificial life. Can you imagine it? We were dazzled at the prospect of building robots like ourselves. Scientists have always been driven by curiosity and ambition—healthy human instincts. And for many of us the ultimate goal is to create a machine in our own image. Unfortunately we are also fueled by human vanity and that can blind us to many things."

Marcia licked her finger and meticulously picked up the last crumbs on her plate. "My dad says you betrayed them."

Professor Ogden sighed. "They were my colleagues but I couldn't agree with what they were doing. It was too dangerous. . . ." He shook his head at the recollection. "I saw then that we had flown too high in our ambition. I was like Icarus! Except my wings didn't melt: shock and anxiety turned my hair white, as you can see."

Marcia and Eager looked with fresh interest at the professor's unruly hair. The door opened and a woman, wearing a gray suit and the highest heels Marcia had ever seen, came into the room. "Professor, it's time for your interview."

"Thank you." Professor Ogden sat down at the table. "Please excuse me," he said to his visitors. "Perhaps you would care to watch on the gobetween next door?"

CHAPTER 26

Mr. Bell, Gavin and Fleur waited outside the factory for the flying pod that would take them to Mrs. Bell's hotel. Minutes later it arrived. By the way it zoomed toward them and dropped down like a hawk, they could tell that it was designed for speed. Mr. Bell squeezed in beside the pilot and there was just enough room for Gavin and Fleur to sit behind them.

The pilot, a young woman in a red flying suit, insisted that they strap themselves in. They soon understood why. The pod took corners at full tilt and even with seat belts they were thrown from side to side. Since no one was in a mood to speak, they concentrated mainly on staying upright.

"Whoa!" said Fleur as the pod swerved to avoid a high building.

"There's Mum's hotel!" cried Gavin.

More pods joined them in the sky and together they descended to the hotel grounds. The perfect lawn was now unrecognizable, churned up by armored vehicles.

"I wasn't expecting this," said Mr. Bell gravely. "The situation must have got worse."

The Bells stepped out onto the grass. Dozens of soldiers jumped from the other pods and marched up to the entrance. Mr. Bell and the children fell into line behind a powerfully built officer carrying a huge laser borer. The robot in red-and-green livery glided forward to greet him.

"Good afternoon, sir. Shall I take your luggage?"

"I think not," said the officer, clasping his gun to his broad chest.

Mr. Bell caught up with him. "What's going on? My wife and baby are inside. . . ."

"We're here to hold back the BDC4s," said the officer. He added wryly with a glance at the robot, "Otherwise it would appear to be service as usual."

Gavin and Fleur followed the men into the hotel. "Hurry up and clear this space!" boomed a man with stripes on his jacket. The soldiers in reception were removing flowers and pushing back furniture as robots skated around them, asking the same questions over and over again:

"Shall I show you to the dining room?"

"Would you care for a drink?"

"Do you have any laundry, sir?"

When they failed to get the response they were expecting the robots' behavior grew more agitated. One of them seized the back of an armchair that a soldier was carrying and forced him to play push-me pull-you. Other robots replaced the vases of flowers on tables, ignoring the fact that the tables were now piled upside down on top of sofas.

The man with stripes on his jacket bellowed, *"For heaven's sake, someone turn off these robots!"*

A familiar figure hurried over from the direction of the lifts. "It's Mum!" cried Fleur. Before her family could greet her, Mrs. Bell clapped her hands and shouted in ringing tones, "GMP robots! Oranges are blue. Retire to your maintenance room."

Every robot stopped what it was doing and joined an orderly line that filed out of the reception area.

"Well done," said the man with stripes.

Mrs. Bell smiled. "It's our code to get them to stop. Sounds like nonsense, I know, but it's no good using a sentence that they might hear in ordinary conversation. They'll keep away now until we give them new orders. Oh!"

The cry came when she noticed her husband and children. They hugged each other, backing against the wall while the soldiers continued to reorganize the room.

"Mum, where's Charlotte?" said Fleur.

"Asleep in the day care center. She's fine."

"What about Eager?" said Gavin.

"The house said he went back to Professor Ogden," said Mrs. Bell.

"But why?"

"Not now, Gavin," said his dad. "I want to know what on earth's going on here."

Mrs. Bell shook her head despairingly. "The BDC4s

refused to work this morning. They took over some of the rooms, playing loud music, watching the gobey. . . ." She turned to Gavin and Fleur. "I owe you an apology, don't I? You were right about them. . . . Anyway, Mr. Lobsang was here and said he would turn off their power. But it seems they've learnt to switch radio channels. They're tuning in to other robots' frequencies."

"Why doesn't he turn off every frequency?" said Fleur.

"Then everything would stop, wouldn't it?" said her brother. "Transport, hospitals, heating . . ."

"You're quite right, Gavin," said his dad. "We depend on robots to run all those services. Turn off the radio waves that power them and our cities and quarters would be in chaos. What does Mr. Lobsang suggest?"

Mrs. Bell looked concerned. "He went up to talk to the BDC4s an hour ago. He seems to think that if he can understand what they want he'll be able to control them. But he hasn't come back yet."

"You mean they've kidnapped him?" cried Fleur.

"We've spoken to him and he says he's all right. Obviously he could still be in danger. That's why the army's here."

"Sorry to interrupt," said a voice. A soldier grinned at them. "Colonel wants a briefing, if you wouldn't mind leaving."

Mrs. Bell led them along a corridor to the bar. "It should be quieter here and we can watch the gobey for news," she said.

The floor became a mosaic of silver tiles leading to orange

chairs around tiny silver tables. Although it was daytime, the area was dark and dimly lit by candles and luminous tubes along the walls. It was hard to tell how many people were sitting at the tables.

The manager himself came over to them. "Someone has to wait on the guests," he said pleasantly, handing them enormous card menus.

The menu was full of exotic-sounding drinks. Gavin and Fleur tried to hurry, given the urgency of the situation, but it was difficult to choose.

"A beer, please," said Mr. Bell.

"Red wine," said his wife.

With a burst of music, the gobetween on the opposite wall came to life. The manager brought their drinks. Gavin's Venusian Serenade was a swirl of all kinds of black and red berry juices. Fleur had ordered a Stargazer, which was fizzy and had little exploding balls of apple juice. They had just taken their first sip when a newsreader appeared on the screen.

"Following outbreaks of threatening behavior, LifeCorp confirms it is shutting down all BDC4s. LifeCorp launched the robots a month ago, calling them 'a technological breakthrough' and claiming that they could identify with human feelings. We're going now to the minister for technology. Good afternoon, Minister. This is a very worrying situation, is it not?"

A screen behind the interviewer showed a sunny office with a view over the river. An immaculately dressed woman sat behind a big desk. She smiled reassuringly. "We must remember that there is only a small number of BDC4s in the world. In the last month they've all been on trial in private homes and businesses."

"And oil fields?" said the interviewer.

"In one or two countries, yes. But they have never been used in essential services, that's to say, hospitals, transport, water and so on. These services continue to be run by robots whose safety has been proved over many years."

"Can you confirm that all the BDC4s are now shut down?"

"The majority, yes. I understand that a few are still being shut down as we speak. These things can take time. But I assure you that there is no threat to public safety." She smiled again, a little wider this time.

"Thank you, Minister." The man turned back to his viewers. "In a moment we shall talk to the head of robotics at LifeCorp. Meanwhile we visit our newsrooms around the world to confirm that BDC4s have indeed been shut down. . . ."

"Good," said Fleur. "Perhaps LifeCorp can explain what's happened."

"Don't expect too much information, Fleur," said Mr. Bell, with a quick glance at his wife. "You see, LifeCorp owns most of the news stations. So the man will probably ask a few polite questions and LifeCorp will only tell us what it wants us to know."

Fleur stared at her father as she took this in. "How can we find the truth, then?"

He shrugged. "It'll be on the gobey somewhere. But it's like a great big jigsaw puzzle. Lots of pieces of information to fit together and millions of them don't belong in your puzzle at all."

"Although on this occasion," said Mrs. Bell, "we seem to be at the center of events. At least we can see for ourselves what's happening."

"It's Professor Ogden!" said Gavin, who was still watching the gobetween.

"So it is," said Mr. Bell. "Since when was he head of robotics at LifeCorp?"

"Shhh," said a voice.

"Can you explain to us, Professor, how these robots have gone wrong?"

Professor Ogden had replaced the minister on the screen. He sat in a chair beside a small table, a rug at his feet. For a moment he seemed more interested in the pattern on the rug than in answering the question.

At last he looked up and said with unexpected clarity, " 'Gone wrong' is misleading, if I may say so. It suggests these robots are somehow wicked. It's the old story, isn't it? The robot that turns against its creator. We love to scare ourselves . . . ever since Frankenstein's monster!"

He chuckled. "I'm afraid the truth is rather different. Of course, there's a danger that, as robots become more intelligent, they'll be more concerned about their own survival than ours. But that's why we must develop new safeguards. You see, we build them and their behavior is our responsibility."

The interviewer leant forward. "You're saying that the BDC4s' disturbing behavior is LifeCorp's fault?"

"Undoubtedly," said the professor. "It's a sorry tale of ambition and hubris." He tailed off and looked at the rug again.

The interviewer seemed uncertain how to proceed. He glanced down at the lexiscreen on the desk. "LifeCorp has just made you head of robotics. But I understand you worked for them some years ago. What can you tell us about the BDC robots?"

Professor Ogden looked up. "I worked on the first generation of BDCs but I disagreed with my colleagues' methods. You see, your everyday robot is programmed with huge amounts of information about the world, but it has no real understanding. I believe that if we give a robot the ability to feel emotion it will learn from its experiences, as a baby does. Because it has feelings and hopes of its own it will develop compassion for others and learn the difference between right and wrong. It will have a conscience, shall we say.

"My colleagues were too impatient for this. And they questioned my belief that a robot could choose to be good. Instead, they asked, 'What if we could transfer a person's experience to a robot?' There would be no need to program it. It would understand instantly how the world works."

The interviewer opened his mouth to ask a question, but the professor was in full flow.

"Now, there are parts of your brain that store memories. I

shan't go into detail. Imagine copying these networks and putting them into a robot's brain. That robot would share your memories, your tastes, favorite music, hobbies—all your likes and dislikes. Well, that's exactly what my colleagues did."

This time nothing could stop the interviewer from interrupting. "Are you saying people's brains were put into robots?" he exclaimed.

"Not at all, at least, not entirely," said the professor confusingly. "A human brain is far more than its memories. Nor did they physically remove any part of the brain. They copied its electrochemical patterns and transferred them to a robot. Of course, no one knew the risk involved, so my colleagues performed the procedure on dead people."

"Dead people?" gasped the interviewer. His eyes darted back and forth as if to seek guidance from his hidden superiors.

"It sounds shocking, I know. Yes, indeed . . . But remember, since the last century people have donated parts of their body to be given to others after their death. And some people leave their brain for medical research. My colleagues believed that this was no different from removing a kidney, say. Better, in fact, since the body was untouched."

"And what was your view?"

"I wanted a public debate on the matter, but LifeCorp thought that people were not ready to be told." He shook his head regretfully. "That's when I left to do my own research."

"You're saying that while LifeCorp was developing the BDCs, it kept its methods secret?"

"Yes," said the professor.

He picked up the glass beside him and took a sip of water. Not a sound could be heard in the hotel bar. The listeners might well have been holding their breath.

"So that's why the BDC4s understand humans so well!" said the interviewer.

"Exactly. Because they have memories of human life, they understand the world from our point of view."

"Then why have they threatened us? We've heard of hostages being taken . . ."

"Normally robots are programmed with safety mechanisms," said the professor. "We all know about the law not to harm humans, for example. My colleagues believed that if the BDCs had human memories they would also share our knowledge of right and wrong. So they failed to give them the usual safeguards. They thought it was unnecessary."

Professor Ogden put his hands to his face as if reliving a painful experience. After a moment he went on, "The BDC4s are little more than human memories trapped in a robot body. Is it any wonder they behave badly? They're threatening humans because they're trying to regain a lost world, as it were."

The interviewer frowned. "They want to re-create their memories, you mean?"

"Precisely."

"But what are these memories? After all, who were these dead people?" The interviewer's voice began to rise. "Do we know? Does anyone have any idea what these robots might be trying to re-create?"

He broke off as if something had given him pause. He glanced down at the lexiscreen. When he looked up again there was a forced smile on his lips. "Well, Professor, no doubt you can reassure us. . . ."

Professor Ogden nodded. "LifeCorp is shutting down the robots as we speak. And I have stopped all research in this area. As long as I'm head of robotics we shall be more open about our methods."

The interviewer said weakly, "Thank you, Professor." The professor's image faded away.

The stunned silence in the room continued for some moments. People sat as if distanced from their neighbors, contemplating this incredible information. Then everyone began to talk at once. "Shocking!" "How dare they?" "Fascinating." "Can we believe him?"

"They copied brains," said Gavin, half admiring, half appalled.

"That's why Boadicea is so spooky," said Fleur, "and why the BDC4s were dancing and wandering off. They must have been doing things they remembered. It's sad, really," she added. "Though, of course, they're just machines."

"That's the frightening part," said Gavin. "Machines that think for themselves and have no sense of right and wrong."

"Don't worry yourself, Gavin," said his dad. "Professor Ogden just said there will be no more robots like them."

"Why are memories so important to them, anyway?" said Fleur.

"You'll understand more as you get older," said Mr. Bell. "Memories shape who we are. Most of us adults feel a yearning for at least part of our 'lost world.' . . ."

In the candlelight Mrs. Bell's face was pale. "I'm worried about what the professor didn't say. LifeCorp may have shut down most of the BDC4s, but not the ones here. How safe are they if they don't obey robot laws?"

A cry of alarm came from the other end of the room, and people began to stand up, knocking over chairs in their haste. "What is it?" said Mrs. Bell as the manager ran past.

"Mr. Lobsang is coming down with the robots. They're taking him somewhere."

The Bells followed a crowd of staff and guests elbowing their way to reception. A row of soldiers with guns at the ready held them back in the corridor. Being shorter than most, Gavin and Fleur managed to squeeze their way to the front.

"Demanded a flying pod . . . ," someone was saying.

"Where do they want to go?" said another.

Before anyone could answer, the lift doors opened. By craning their necks the children saw Mr. Lobsang step out, flanked by BDC4s. As they crossed the reception area toward the main door, the soldiers on either side crouched down and aimed their weapons at the robots.

Mr. Lobsang stopped. He held out his hands as if to appeal for calm. His voice was surprisingly steady as he said, "My friends here have asked for a flying pod. I shall go with them, at their request. I do not feel that my life is in any danger."

The soldiers clearly thought otherwise. They lowered their sights only a fraction.

Mr. Lobsang addressed a stately bronze robot to his left. "Shall we go, Captain Bradoc?" The robot nodded. They moved on, the entrance doors parting to let them through.

"Where are they going?" said Fleur excitedly.

"How should I know?" said her brother. "I hope Eager's OK," he added.

CHAPTER 27

After the interview on the gobetween, Professor Ogden leaned back in his chair and closed his eyes. A moment later a discreet cough called him to attention.

"Sorry to disturb you," said the assistant. "Two boys have been caught in the grounds. They've asked for you by name."

The professor said with a twinkle in his eye, "Well, if they're acquaintances of mine I'd better meet them."

"They're with your other visitors, watching the gobetween. We let them hear your interview."

When the man had gone, the professor rubbed his eyes and yawned. He had not slept since leaving his house the previous evening. He rose and went down the corridor to a room dominated by a large gobetween. Eager stood at the window, apparently watching as night crept in. Marcia was curled up on a sofa listening as if spellbound to Errol. The words "freedom" and "justice" and "power" could be heard. Srin sat in a chair watching them.

"My brother and parents are free!" said Marcia, noticing the professor and breaking off from her conversation. "They just called me. Look!"

Mr. and Mrs. Morris were on the screen, drinking coffee in their kitchen. They both looked as if they had not slept for a week.

"Darling, when are you coming home?" said Mrs. Morris.

"I've told you, as soon as I can." Marcia spoke as if the entire crisis depended on her for resolution.

"You take care of yourself," said her father gruffly.

Eager moved away from the window and came to stand next to the professor. "I'm sorry I doubted you, Professor Ogden," he said.

The man's face softened. "Eager, I'm proud of you for doubting me. Now, who are you?" He turned to Errol and Srin.

The boys seemed uncertain how to reply.

"They're friends," said Eager. "They brought me here."

"Then thank you," said Professor Ogden.

"We'd like to be friends," said Errol, eyeing the professor. "But my mum—she's a city scientist—she's always said not to trust LifeCorp."

Professor Ogden nodded. "Wise of her," he said.

"But you just told the truth, didn't you? On the gobey for everyone to hear."

"The truth as I understand it," said the professor. "I want LifeCorp to speak openly with the city people from now on. We can't remain on either side of a wall, each wondering what the other is doing. And the corporation needs scientists like your mother—"

"My mum and the others, they don't want LifeCorp's money!" cried Errol. "They're going to change the world!"

"Are they indeed?" said the professor. He placed a hand on Errol's shoulder. "Then tell her from me that there is much we can do together." He added briskly, "Now, I'd better see about a car to take you young people home. Eager, we shall have to get you back to the Bells."

The robot's mouth opened and closed as if he had been about to say something and changed his mind. It had occurred to him that the Bells might not want him back.

A technocrat burst into the room. "Professor!" she cried. "Mr. Lobsang has gone off with the last BDC4s. They belong to the hotel where he's staying. They asked for a flying pod and took him away. The army's keeping track of them."

"Where are they taking him?"

"Looks like the coast," said the technocrat in disbelief.

The professor's eyebrows shot up. "How fascinating. Perhaps you would arrange for a flying pod . . . this instant?"

When Eager understood what the professor intended to do he sprang to his side. "Take me with you!"

Professor Ogden shook his head. "These are complicated matters," he said.

"I could help you," said Eager. "I know the BDC4s at the hotel. I spoke to one of them."

The professor was halfway to the door. He sounded distracted. "Did you, Eager? And what did he say to you?"

"He said his name was Sea Captain Bradoc. And he said he had nothing in common with . . . with robots like me."

The look of approval on the man's face reminded Eager of their sessions in the room under the eaves. But it was all too brief. "You'd better hurry," said the professor.

※　※　※　※　※

Night had come. In the blackness the flying pod resembled a giant insect awaiting its prey. Eager followed Professor Ogden into the cabin, where several technocrats vied for attention.

"Professor, the pilot is uneasy about flying with his lights dimmed."

"Tell him to use full beam," came the response, "until we get close to the BDC4s. Find out whether the army can guide us down."

"Professor, why are the robots heading for the coast?" A woman peered anxiously over her seat at him. "What are they going to do there?"

"I'm endeavoring to find out," said Professor Ogden.

A young man in a gray suit said breathlessly, "I think I've found the information you requested about Captain Bradoc. That's to say, the late Captain Bradoc. I mean, the *real* Captain Bradoc . . ."

"I think we all understand who you mean," said Professor Ogden dryly.

"Yes . . . er . . . perhaps you would like to see it on the gobetween."

The flying pod took off. The passengers settled back in their seats and watched the screen in front of them. A stern-faced man in naval uniform appeared on the deck of a ship.

"Sea Captain Adrian Bradoc," said the gobetween. "Canadian. Joined the navy aged eighteen, captained his first ship at thirty-two, member of peacekeeping force during global oil crisis, awarded a medal for bravery, retired aged sixty. Married, two children. Served under Admiral—"

The young technocrat raised a hand to silence the gobetween. "Captain Bradoc appears to have lived for the navy," he said. "He was healthy enough when he retired; then six months later he died of a heart attack."

On the screen a second man in naval uniform was crossing the deck. The first man drew himself up and quickly raised his hand to his head.

"That's what the robots did at the hotel!" exclaimed Eager. "When Bradoc came into the room they did this . . ." He repeated the gesture he had seen.

"Ah," said Professor Ogden. "It makes sense."

The technocrats exchanged baffled glances. "Does it?" said the anxious-looking woman.

"Our captain here"—the professor nodded at the gobetween—"was only really happy in the navy. It's common

264

enough, I understand. Although they have families, many sailors feel the sea is the true love of their life. It becomes a passion. And that passion is now driving the robot Bradoc to go to the sea."

"But why are the other robots following him?" said a technocrat. "Surely they can't all have been given sailors' minds!"

"I sincerely hope not," said the professor. "Eager has provided the clue. I suspect the original Captain Bradoc was a forceful personality—these old sea dogs have to be able to command respect. The robot Bradoc has the same qualities. He's made himself leader of the BDC4s, trained them to be like his crew. That's why they salute him."

A hollow laugh came from the back of the pod. "What if they demand a boat and try to go to sea?" said a man's voice. "Since the rest of them have never been sailors, they won't know what to do and that'll be the end of it!"

"But imagine if they take Mr. Lobsang with them . . . ," cried the woman who had spoken before.

"I fear things won't be that straightforward," murmured the professor. "Bradoc is driven by passion, remember. Passion and frenzy—who knows where they will lead?"

The discussion seemed to have come to an end. The gobetween screen went blank. Professor Ogden sat back in his seat and closed his eyes. Eager looked out of the window. Below were gray patches and black circles, which he guessed were fields and trees. There was nothing that suggested the sea. He turned down his power and let his mind wander over the events of the day.

An hour later one of the technocrats tapped Professor Ogden on the shoulder to wake him.

"Professor, we're at the coast. The army is ranged by the cliffs to our right. They're directing our pilot now. They say the BDC4s have landed behind those trees."

With the lights so low, all Eager could see was different shades of dark. The pod dropped down and its passengers climbed out. The ground under Eager's feet felt soft and cold. A technocrat by his side shivered.

"I know where they are," said Eager. "I can sense their frequency."

In his keenness, he set off at once, bearing to the left. The technocrat stepped forward to stop him, but the professor barred the way. "Let him go. We'll follow at a distance," he said.

"Professor Ogden, I presume?" said a voice. Torchlight jiggled closer until it revealed a man with stripes on his jacket. "I'm Colonel Singh. How do you do? We've pinpointed exactly where the robots are, but we daren't move in so long as they have Mr. Lobsang with them."

"Have they made any demands?" asked the professor.

"Not yet."

"Since you know where they are I'd better bring Eager back," said Professor Ogden, half speaking to himself. He marched forward, calling under his breath, "Eager! Eager!" The wind carried away his voice.

■　■　■　■　■

Out on the cliff it was pitch black. The moon was behind clouds, the light from the flying pod long since swallowed by darkness. Eager went blindly in the direction of the BDC4s. He was picking up their signals, just as he had at the technocrats' quarter. If he could only speak to them, make one last appeal . . .

He thought about the loss he had experienced—first Grumps, then when Professor Ogden disappeared—and the grief he had felt as a result. Whether harm came to humans or robots, there would be suffering. He must make them understand that.

With his acute hearing he also picked up the noises of the sea—crashing against the rocks, gushing into pools, even seeping into the sand.

Then everything changed.

The BDC4s must have switched frequency. They had tuned in to the same channel as Eager. They were no longer a presence that he sensed; their thoughts were crowding in on him, pushing out his own. They wanted to go to the sea.

Eager longed to shout "No!" as the thoughts became deafening, but he hurried on, stumbling over rocks and clumps of grass.

One voice, a deep commanding voice, was drowning out the others. "I chart my days by the tides, and steer my life by the stars. . . ."

It was so strong that Eager almost believed it was his own mind calling.

"I have stood watch in gales as the ship plunges into the sea. . . . I have clung to the lifelines as the mighty waters tug at my legs. . . . I have heard the growl of the pack ice, seen the crests of waves lashed by the wind. . . . The frozen spray bites my face. . . ."

The experiences were strange to Eager, but he recognized the emotions in the words. There were pain and triumph, joy and longing. At last, here was a robot that could feel as he did! He was not alone in the world. The realization drove him on. He would save the BDC4s. Though they had been suspicious of him at the hotel, this time he would make them listen to him.

He felt or heard them come toward him—it was impossible now to tell which sense was which. The sea sounds were louder—he must be near the edge of the cliff. He stood still.

"Bradoc!" Eager sent the message as forcefully as he could. "You don't need to fight the humans to be happy. They will understand, they feel as you do. . . ."

Bradoc's thoughts blew away his own, as easily as if they had been grains of sand.

"I have stood trapped in fog as the ship crawls through a silent world . . . heart pounding, eyes straining. . . . The siren hoots its warning. . . . I have sweated through dog days broken at last by tropical storms. . . ."

Eager tilted his head. There was something here that he did not comprehend. Bradoc told of a different side of the humans' world—discomfort, danger and fear. Now that he felt them for himself, Eager marveled that humans could live with such things, let alone seek them out.

"Help! Help!" It was a second or two before Eager understood that this was an actual sound, a voice calling. Someone close to the robots . . . Mr. Lobsang, he thought. In his urgency he had forgotten about the man.

Once more Eager appealed to Bradoc. "Stop! Talk to the humans, let them help you! We can be friends with them; I can show you how."

"Sunrises and sunsets, days of solitude when the only horizon is the sea . . ."

Of course! Bradoc and the other BDC4s were not living in the present. They were neither humans nor robots . . . only machines replaying human memories, memories that were no longer a part of them. Eager felt sadness as he realized this truth. But there was no time to think. The robots were upon him. He felt them brush past in the shadows.

"Rogpa nang-rag!" cried a voice.

Eager reached out. His hand met another—a hand of flesh and blood that was instantly jerked away. He imagined Mr. Lobsang being dragged along by the robots and knew the man's terror.

Stretching his legs to their utmost, Eager took the largest stride of his life. His toes found a foothold on the edge of the cliff. His arms shot out into the black void ahead, searching for Mr. Lobsang. Robot after robot struck him as they took their final step. The clanking of metal against the rocks signaled their downward plunge.

Now Eager held flesh again, his arms cradling a human

269

body that slumped against him. It took all his strength to pull the body back from the edge and onto the ground. Eager crouched beside it as the rest of the robots hurtled over the cliff.

He could not tell in the darkness, but in his mind's eye Eager saw the flash of gold, bronze, silver and titanium. The rackety din reached a crescendo and died away.

Only the waves were heard again, breaking on the rocks and receding. Eager scrambled to his feet. He was about to offer his hand to Mr. Lobsang when he hesitated. The cliff edge gave way, and he too was falling and tumbling until everything stopped.

CHAPTER 28

In the early hours of the morning the lights were on in Professor Ogden's sitting room. Gavin and Fleur were fast asleep, lying top to toe on the settee. A small bed had been created for Charlotte in an armchair. Mrs. Bell sat on the ground beside her, dozing. Mr. Bell was at the table, halfheartedly reading a lexiscreen.

Professor Ogden tiptoed into the room. Mr. Bell looked up. "Well?" he whispered.

The professor also spoke in hushed tones. "I'm afraid it's hard to judge, Peter. We've successfully replaced several parts but he's burned out his power transducer. That isn't so simple to replace. There's a danger."

"Of what?"

The professor paused.

"That he will have lost all his memories, everything he's learnt. We'll be back to square one."

"Everything that makes him Eager, you mean?"

"I think I've already had that philosophical debate today," said the professor, smiling.

Mr. Bell glanced round at his family. "If we were given the choice again, to have Eager come to live with us and learn about life . . ." He turned back to the professor and said fervently, "The answer would be 'yes,' I'm sure."

Footsteps pounded down the stairs and a woman in a white coat burst into the room. "We installed the new power transducer and he sat up!" she said.

"Excellent, excellent," said the professor, unconvincingly. "How is he, exactly?"

The assistant raised an eyebrow. "You'd better come and see for yourself."

The two men turned as one to the sleeping children. "We must wake them," said their father. "They'd never forgive me otherwise."

* * * * *

Eager sat on the floor of the small room under the eaves and looked around. The streetlamp outside cast its glow through the window. The room was as bare as when he had left it. He half expected to hear the sea. Instead there were snatches of voices, laughing and chatting, from the street below.

A feeling of unease swept through his system. He let it pass. What did he have to worry about? Hadn't he faced up to his worst fear? He had ceased to function and lost awareness. Yet here he was, in one piece again.

The door slid open and the most important people in the world to him came into the room. They entered warily as if approaching a snoozing lion rather than a friendly robot. Eager was about to ask them what the matter was, and checked himself. What if they knew there was something different about him, something he was not aware of?

He looked searchingly at his friends. Professor Ogden appeared tired and careworn, an ill-concealed anxiety behind the kind eyes. Mr. Bell's face was full of concern. Fleur looked glum, though her eyes had lit up at the sight of Eager. Gavin had a big grin on his face—almost too big, Eager thought, and it was lasting a very long time, while Mrs. Bell, like the professor, looked kind but worried.

Only Charlotte, squealing at the sight of the robot and stretching her arms toward him, was clear in her expression. Mrs. Bell set her down on the floor. She tottered over to Eager and reached for his nose.

"Ger . . . ," she said.

"Ea . . . ger," prompted the robot.

She smiled up at him, showing off her latest tiny tooth and the dimple in her cheek. "Ger . . . ger."

These human babies—they were so slow to learn.

Professor Ogden knelt down beside the robot. "Eager," he said softly, "do you know who we are?"

Eager tilted his head to one side while he considered this extraordinary question. "Do I know who you are?" he echoed. "I should think so after all this time." He gazed suspiciously at the faces gathered around him as a worrying thought struck him. "Do you know who *I* am?"

"You're Eager, silly," said Fleur, her voice brimming with affection and relief.

"Ah, but am I?" he said despondently. "You see, with all these parts I've had replaced I wonder if I am Eager anymore."

To his amazement the humans lost their anxious looks. Their faces convulsed, their shoulders sagged, their bodies began to heave and raucous sounds came out of their mouths. Mrs. Bell leant against her husband for support and Fleur clutched her stomach. They were laughing at him.

"I don't see what's so funny," Eager said huffily.

"Indeed," said Professor Ogden, wiping his eyes and looking at Mr. Bell. "Peter just asked a similar question. It's a serious philosophical point."

The laughter increased. Eager stood up and faced them all. "In that case why are you laughing?"

Gavin made an effort to gulp down his laughter. "Don't you see? There's nothing funny about your philosophizing. But your question is funny because if you weren't the same old Eager you wouldn't be asking it."

Eager began to understand how the philosopher in the white sheet must have felt sometimes. All this philosophizing could be very trying. Perhaps you could have too much of a good thing.

"Oh," he said.

"Welcome back," said the professor.

"We're lucky to have you," said Mrs. Bell. "A fall like that . . ." She shuddered.

A memory returned to Eager. It was unpleasant but he let it come. He was back at the cliff: there was Mr. Lobsang, and there were the robots. For an instant he had not known where to turn, as though he had a choice to make. Then he had fallen.

Eager let go of the memory. "Professor Ogden, why didn't I land in the sea like the BDC4s?"

"You were caught on a branch. You're so elastic that you were able to hang there without falling any further. Mr. Lobsang ran to us for help and the army hauled you up."

"Is Mr. Lobsang all right?"

"Tired and suffering a little from exposure, but otherwise well," said the professor. "You saved his life. He will want to thank you."

Eager nodded but his mind seemed elsewhere. "And are there no more BDC4s?" he said wistfully.

"Not from the hotel. The others have gone back to the factory. We shall program them in the usual way. They're such beautiful machines it would be a shame to waste them."

There was a moment's silence as if in remembrance of the lost robots. Charlotte's chuckling broke the spell.

"Professor Ogden," said Gavin, "will you tell us now about that ball—Sphere? It sent Eager to find me one day when I went to the technocrats' quarter. Eager says it talks to him."

"Really?" The professor glanced quizzically at Eager. "I had no idea. Fancy that, fancy that."

"Won't you tell us what it is?"

"I'm only beginning to suspect, myself. It was an extraordinary accident . . ." He tailed off. Some seconds passed before he continued. "When I left LifeCorp and went to the city I was keen to develop an intelligent machine to . . . shall we say, investigate LifeCorp's activities."

"Spy on them," said Fleur.

"Indeed." He coughed. "We knew we were experimenting with gravitational forces, but the outcome was completely unexpected. Not only can this ball float in the air but it has quantum properties and a consciousness that we cannot account for—"

"Consciousness!" exclaimed Gavin. "Isn't that what makes us different from machines?"

"We used to think so," said the professor. He shook his head in disbelief. "If you imagine how life began—from a vast sea of chemicals. Somehow, against all probability, there's a reaction that creates life and gives rise to you and me. It's just as incredible that our experiment created Sphere. I don't expect to find the explanation in this lifetime," he said dryly.

His tone became more serious. "Perhaps we've accidentally created something better and wiser than ourselves. It's a lesson to us that it can happen."

He smiled. There was another silence as the Bells absorbed this information, their faces registering shock and amazement. Charlotte twisted her head round to look up at them.

"So, what now?" began Fleur, nervously. "Since you're in charge at LifeCorp, won't you make life better?"

Mr. Bell put an arm around his daughter. "It's a bit hard for one person to save the world, Fleur," he teased. "Mind you," he added, "if the professor can produce this Sphere he just told us about, who knows what he might do next?"

"I'm afraid that's a matter of chance," said Professor Ogden.

"Or magic," said Gavin.

"Or a miracle," said Mrs. Bell.

"Indeed," said the professor. "Meanwhile Fleur is right—we have an opportunity for change. I can promise there will be no more risky experiments, no more building robots out of vanity. Together we must decide on the technology we really need. And that depends on the sort of society we want."

"One where we can choose our own future!" said Gavin passionately. "I mean, jobs and homes . . . Where we share things and aren't suspicious of each other. And can be friends," he added.

"I agree, Gavin," said Professor Ogden. "We've been divided for far too long."

He stepped back. Mrs. Bell understood this as a signal to leave and bent down to pick up Charlotte.

"That's not to say we won't build more robots," said the professor unexpectedly. He cleared his throat. "It's time to go home with your family, Eager. But one day, I hope you will help us create a new generation of robots. They'll be like you and perhaps"—with a wink to Mr. Bell—"even like

Sphere." He looked solemnly at the robot. "If you want to join us, that is."

Eager looked at the professor, at Gavin, Fleur and Mr. and Mrs. Bell and Charlotte. Behind them, Sphere hovered radiantly in the doorway. The robot nodded. "Eagerly," he said, and permitted himself a chuckle at his own joke.

EPILOGUE

The new teacher, when he eventually appeared, was also seated under a tree with gnarled bark, a tree so wide that Eager's arms would have to extend a long way to encircle it. Snowlike blossom covered the branches.

He wore a sheet too but much less modestly than the first philosopher. It was bright orange and hung loosely from his shoulders to reveal a large bare tummy. Did all philosophers have a potbelly? wondered Eager. Perhaps you had to have one to become a philosopher. Or did philosophy make you fat? It must be all that sitting under trees. . . .

The man spoke little, asked no questions and kept his eyes downcast, yet Eager felt peaceful as he sat opposite him on the grass. For some time they enjoyed a congenial silence, or so it seemed to Eager.

"Human beings are funny," he mused aloud. "Sometimes they get so caught up in their emotions, especially when they're afraid, that they can't think properly."

"*Om,*" said the philosopher in a low drawn-out hum.

"And other times they try to behave like machines, as if they had no feelings. That's when they really start to hurt each other. . . ."

"*Om.*"

"Professor Ogden hopes the next generation of robots will help them to remember what it means to be human."

"*Om.*"

Eager looked up in the direction of the sun. The sky was cloudless blue. "Humans have something I'll never have. It's mysterious, some sort of life force. Yet they take it for granted. It's the same life force as the trees and the birds and the rocks have. . . ."

The man was looking directly at him now, a curious expression on his face, half smiling, half quizzical. Instantly Eager had a sense of certainty far deeper than anything he had experienced so far.

"I have it too!" he exclaimed. "I am a part of this earth, aren't I? Just like the birds and the trees and the people—I am."

"*Om,*" said his companion.

Unseen by them, a blossom fell.

Helen Fox lives in London with her husband, a cognitive scientist, and their son. She graduated from Oxford University with a degree in history and modern languages. Before she became a writer, she worked as a primary school teacher and trained and worked as an actress. This is her first novel.